WHAT THE C   ) & JULIET:

"Intelligent, lighthearted and entertaining" – *New York Times Book Review*

"An outstanding talent for comic scenes" – *The Observer*

"Utterly charming and hilarious" – *Sunday Independent*

"An immensely pleasurable read" – *RTE Guide*

"A superb first novel" – *Belfast Newsletter*

"Exudes grace and warmth... *Juno & Juliet* is the most brutally and hilariously real depiction of Irish undergraduate and academic life since *The Ginger Man*." – *LA Times*

"Hugely entertaining... Gough, who has already been compared to Roddy Doyle in his feel for the tempo and texture of Irish city life, has created an unforgettable narrator in Juliet Taylor: through her smart, sensitive gaze, ordinary events take on an almost epic quality." – *Vogue*

"A great read, a page-turner, and funny too - what more could you ask?" – *Northern Woman*

"As charming as puppies, and often very funny" – *Big Issue*

"Julian Gough is like Roddy Doyle in an extremely good mood... There's a lot to be said for happiness, and the author here offers us a dazzling defence of joy." – *Washington Post*

"Upbeat, optimistic and funny" – *Hello!*

"A modern, at times brilliantly ironic reworking of the classical fairy tale, with nods to Shakespeare, Austen and Beckett." − *Literary Review*

"Guaranteed to make both literary luvvies and light readers melt... Intelligent and deliciously dry, Gough's sparkling words can't fail to make you sit up, listen and laugh." − *Glamour*

"A polished debut, somewhere between − if you'll pardon the soundbite − Austen and Auster." − *Hotpress*

"Upbeat, action-packed and funny... Gough has created a vivid, memorable supporting cast." − *The List*

"Anyone who has enjoyed the works of Austen will be charmed by this book... Loosely following the plot of *Emma*, Gough's modern-day tale of growing up incorporates all of the essential (and most enjoyable) elements of any Austenian novel - mystery, romance and a happy resolution." − *Sunday Tribune*

"Incredibly life-affirming" − *Impact*

"A triumph" − *Woman's Way*

"Julian Gough has a fantastic talent. I dare anyone not to love this book. I dare anyone to try to borrow this book, it's staying put on my shelves. Great writer, great story, great reading." − *Bassline & Blank Magazine*

"Julian Gough is not a novelist" − *New York Times*

Jude:

Level 1

Jude:

Level 1

Julian Gough

Copyright © Julian Gough 2007

First published in the United Kingdom in 2007 by
Old Street Publishing Ltd, 14 Bowling Green Lane,
London EC1R 0BD, UK
www.oldstreetpublishing.co.uk

Paperback ISBN-13: 978 1 905847 24 2
Hardback ISBN-13: 978 1 905847 33 4

10 9 8 7 6 5 4 3 2 1

A CIP catalogue record for this book is available from the British Library. The
CIP (Cataloguing In Publication) program is not to be confused with the
better known CIP (Centro Internacional de la Papa, or International Potato
Centre), based in La Molina, outside Lima, Peru.

This book is sold subject to the condition that it shall not, by way of trade
or otherwise, be lent, re-sold, hired out, swapped for food, placed in a canoe,
flown in the manner of a kite, or otherwise circulated without the publisher's
prior consent, in any form or binding or cover other than that in which it
is published and without a similar condition including this condition being
imposed on the subsequent purchaser.

All of the people, living, dead, famous, infamous, known and unknown in this
book are fictional or used in a fictional context in a fictional world which
comments on but which is not our own.

Except Jude. Jude is real.

Printed in Finland

This book is dedicated to my parents, Richard Gough and Elizabeth Gough (née Grogan), with love, respect and thanks.

IRELAND

Border Violations

Tipperary	*3*
Galway	*43*
Dublin	*123*

IRELAND

Border Violations

"All ships are safe in harbour.

But that's not what ships are for."

-Unknown

TIPPERARY

1.

If I had urinated immediately after breakfast, the Mob would never have burnt down the Orphanage. But, as I left the dining hall to relieve myself, the letterbox clattered. I turned in the long corridor. A single white envelope lay on the doormat.

I hesitated, and heard through the door the muffled roar of a motorcycle starting. With a crunching turn on the gravel drive and a splatter of pebbles against the door, it was gone.

Odd, I thought, for the postman has a bicycle. I walked to the large oak door, picked up the envelope, and gazed upon it.

Jude
The Orphanage
Tipperary
Ireland

For me! On this day, of all significant days! I sniffed both sides of the smooth white envelope, in the hope of detecting a woman's perfume, or a man's cologne. It smelt, faintly, of itself.

I pondered. I was unaccustomed to letters, never having received one before, and I did not wish to use this one up in the One Go. As I stood in silent thought, I could feel the Orphanage Coffee burning relentlessly through my small dark passages. Should I open the letter before, or after, urinating? It was a dilemma. I wished to open it immediately. But a full bladder distorts judgement when reading, and is a great obstacle to understanding.

Yet could I do justice to my very dilemma, with a full bladder?

As I pondered, both dilemma and letter were removed from my hands by the Master of Orphans, Brother Madrigal.

"You've no time for that now, boy," he said. "Run off and organise the Honour Guard, and get them out to the site. You may open your letter this evening, in my presence, after the Visit." He gazed at my letter with its handsome handwriting, and thrust it up the sleeve of his cassock.

I sighed, and went to find the young Orphans of the Honour Guard.

2.

I found most of the young Orphans hiding under Brother Thomond in the darkness of the hay barn.

"Excuse me, Sir," I said, lifting his skirts and ushering out the protesting infants.

"He is Asleep," said a young Orphan, and indeed, as I looked closer, I saw Brother Thomond was at a slight tilt. Supported from behind by a pillar, he was maintained erect only by the stiffness of his ancient joints. Golden straws protruded from the neck and sleeves of his long black cassock, and emerged at all angles from his wild white hair.

"He said he wished to speak to you, Jude," said another

Orphan. I hesitated. We were already late. I decided not to wake him, for Brother Thomond, once he had Stopped, took a great deal of time to warm up and get rightly going again.

"Where is Agamemnon?" I asked.

The smallest Orphan removed one thumb from his mouth and jerked it upward, towards the loft.

"Agamemnon!" I called softly.

Old Agamemnon, my dearest companion and the Orphanage Pet, emerged slowly from the shadows of the loft and stepped, with a tread remarkably dainty for a dog of such enormous size, down the wooden ladder to the ground. He shook his great ruff of yellow hair and yawned at me loudly.

"Walkies," I said, and he stepped up to my side. We exited the hay barn into the golden light of a perfect Tipperary summer's day.

I lined up the Honour Guard and counted them by the front door, in the shadow of the South Tower of the Orphanage. The butter-yellow bricks of its facade glowed in the diffuse morning light as a late fog burned off.

I checked I had my Travel Toothbrush tucked safely into my sock.

We set out.

3.

From the gates of the Orphanage to the site of the speeches was several strong miles.

We passed through Town, and out the other side. The smaller Orphans began to wail, afraid they would see Black People, or be savaged by Beasts. Agamemnon stuck closely to my rear. We walked until we ran out of road. Then we followed a track, till we ran out of track.

We hopped over a fence, crossed a field, waded a dyke, cut through a ditch, traversed scrub land, forded a river and entered Nobber Nolan's bog. Spang plumb in the middle of Nobber Nolan's Bog, and therefore spang plumb in the middle of Tipperary, and thus Ireland, was the Nation's most famous Boghole, famed in song and story, in History book and Ballad sheet: the most desolate place in Ireland, and the last place God created.

I had never seen the famous boghole, for Nobber Nolan had, until his recent death and his bequest of the Bog to the State, guarded it fiercely from locals and tourists alike. Many's the American was winged with birdshot over the years, attempting to make pilgrimage here. I looked about me for the Hole, but it was hid from my view by an enormous Car-Park, a concrete Interpretive Centre of imposing dimensions, and a tall, broad, wooden stage, or platform, bearing Politicians. Beyond Car-Park and Interpretive Centre, an eight-lane motorway of almost excessive straightness stretched clean to the Horizon, in the direction of Dublin.

Facing the stage stood fifty thousand farmers.

We made our way through the farmers to the stage. They parted politely, many raising their hats, and seemed in high good humour. "'Tis better than the Radio Head concert at Punchestown," said a sophisticated farmer from Cloughjordan, pulling on a shop-bought cigarette.

Onstage, I counted the smaller Orphans. We had lost only the one, which was good going over such a quantity of rough ground. I reported our arrival to Teddy "Noddy" Nolan, the Fianna Fáil TD for Tipperary Central and a direct descendant of Neddy "Nobber" Nolan. Nodding vigorously, he waved us to our places, high at the back of the sloping stage. The Guard of Honour lined up in front of the enormous green cloth backdrop and stood to attention, flanked by groups of seated dignitaries. I myself sat where I could unobtrusively supervise, in a vacant seat at the end of a row.

6

When the last of the stragglers had arrived in the crowd below us, Teddy cleared his throat. The crowd fell silent, as though shot. He began his speech.

"It was in this place..." he said, with a generous gesture which incorporated much of Tipperary, "... that Eamonn DeValera..."

Everybody removed their hats.

"... hid heroically from the Entire British Army..."

Everybody scowled and put their hats back on.

"... during the War of Independence. It was in this very boghole that Eamonn DeValera..."

Everybody removed their hats again.

"... had his Vision: A Vision of Irish Maidens dancing barefoot at the crossroads, and of Irish Manhood dying heroically while refusing to the last breath to buy English shoes..."

At the word English the crowd put their hats back on, though some took them off again when it turned out only to be shoes. Others glared at them. They put the hats back on again.

"We in Tipperary have fought long and hard to get the Government to make Brussels pay for this fine Interpretive Centre and its fine Car-Park, and in Brünhilde DeValera we found the ideal Minister to fight our corner. It is therefore with great pleasure, with great *pride*, that I invite the great grand-daughter of Eamonn DeValera's cousin ... the Minister for Beef, Culture and the Islands ... Brünhilde DeValera ... to officially reopen ... Dev's Hole!"

The crowd roared and waved their hats in the air. Long experience had taught them to keep a firm grip on the peak, for as all the hats were of the same design and entirely indistinguishable, the One from the Other, it was common practice at a Fianna Fáil hat-flinging rally for the less scrupulous farmers to loft an Old Hat, yet pick up a New.

Brünhilde DeValera took the microphone, tapped it, and cleared her throat.

"Spit on me, Brünhilde!" cried an excitable farmer down

the front. The crowd surged forward, toppling and trampling the feeble-legged and bock-kneed, in expectation of Fiery Rhetoric. She began.

"Although it is European Money which has paid for this fine Interpretive Centre... Although it is European Money which has paid for this fine new eight-lane Motorway from Dublin, this Coach Park, this Car Park, that has Tarmacadamed Toomevara in its Entirety... Although it is European Money which has paid for everything built West of Grafton Street in my Lifetime... And although we are grateful to Europe for its Largesse..."

She paused to draw a great Breath. The crowd were growing restless, not having a Bull's Notion where she was going with all this, and distressed by the use of a foreign word.

"It is not for this I brought my Hat," said the Dignitary next to me, and spat on the foot of the Dignitary beside him.

"Nonetheless," said Brünhilde DeValera, "Grateful as we are to the Europeans...

...we should never forget...

...that...

...they..."

Fifty thousand right hands began to drift, with a wonderful easy slowness, up towards the brims of fifty thousand Hats in anticipation of a Climax.

"...are a shower of Foreign Bastards who would Murder us in our Beds given Half a Chance!"

A great cheer went up and the air was filled with Hats till they hid the face of the sun and we cheered in an eerie half-light.

The minister paused for some minutes while everybody recovered their own Hat and returned it to their own Head.

"Those Foreign Bastards in Brussels think they can buy us with their money! They are Wrong! Wrong! Wrong! You cannot buy an Irishman's Heart, an Irishman's Soul, an Irishman's Loyalty! Remember '98!"

There was a hesitation in the crowd, as the younger farmers

tried to remember 1998 but narrowly failed, for that year had not quite arrived yet.

"1798!" Brünhilde clarified.

A great cheer went up as we recalled the gallant failed rebellion of 1798. "Was It For This That Wolfe Tone Died?" came a whisp of song from the back of the crowd.

"Remember 1803!"

We applauded Emmet's great failed rebellion of 1803. A quavering chorus came from the oldest farmers at the rear of the great crowd: "Bold Robert Emmet, the darling of Ireland…"

"Remember 1916!"

Grown men wept as they recalled the great failed rebellion of 1916, and so many contradictory songs were started that none got rightly going.

There was a pause.

All held their breath.

"…Remember 1988!"

Pride so great it felt like anguish filled our hearts as we recalled the year Ireland finally threw off her shackles and stood proud among the community of nations, with our heroic victory over England in the first match in Group Two of the Group Stage of the European Football Championship Finals. A brief chant went up from the Young Farmers in the Mosh Pit: "Who put the ball in the England net?"

Older farmers, further back, added bass to the reply of "Houghton! Houghton!"

I shifted uncomfortably in my seat.

"My great grand-father's cousin did not Fight and Die in bed of old age so that foreign monkey-men could swing from our trees and rape our women! He did not walk out of the Daíl, start a Civil War and kill Michael Collins so a bunch of dirty Foreign Bastards could…"

Here I missed a number of Fiery Words, as excited farmers began to leap up and down roaring at the front, the younger and more nimble mounting each other's shoulders, then throwing themselves forward to surf toward the stage on a sea of hands, holding their Hats on as they went.

"Never forget," roared Brünhilde DeValera, "that a Vision of Ireland came out of Dev's Hole!"

"Dev's Hole! Dev's Hole! Dev's Hole!" roared the crowd.

By my side, Agamemnon began to howl, and tried to dig a hole in the stage with his long claws.

Neglecting to empty my bladder after breakfast had been an error the awful significance of which I only now began to grasp. A good Fianna Fáil Ministerial speech to a loyal audience in the heart of a Tipperary bog could go on for up to five hours.

I pondered my situation.

My only choice seemed to be as to precisely how I would disgrace myself in front of thousands. To rise and walk off the stage during a speech by a semi-descendant of DeValera would be tantamount to treason, and would earn me a series of beatings on my way to the portable toilets.

Yet the alternative was to relieve myself into my breeches where I sat.

My waist-band creaked.

With the gravest reluctance, I willed the loosening of my urethral sphincter.

4.

Nothing happened. My subsequent efforts, over the next few minutes, to void my bladder, resulted only in the vigorous exercising of my superficial abdominal muscles. At length, I realised that there was a fundamental setting in my Subconscious, and it was set firmly against public voidance. To this adamant subconscious setting, my Conscious Mind had no access.

Meanwhile, the pressure grew intolerable, as the Orphanage Coffee continued to bore through my system.

I grew desperate. Yet, within the line of sight of fifty thousand farmers, I could not unleash the torrent.

Then, Inspiration! The Velvet Curtain! All I needed was an instant's distraction, and I could step behind the billowing green backdrop beside me, and vanish. There would, no doubt, be an exit off the back of the stage, through which I could pass to relieve myself, before returning, unobserved, to my place.

A magnificent gust of Nationalist Rhetoric lifted every hat again aloft and, in the moment of eclipse, I stood, took one step sideways, and vanished behind the Curtain.

5.

I shuffled along, my face to the Emerald Curtain, my rear to the rough wooden back wall of the stage, until the wall ceased. I turned, and I beheld, to my astonished delight, the solution to all my problems.

Hidden from stage and crowd by the vast Curtain was a magnificent circular long-drop toilet of the type employed in the Orphanage. But where we sat around a splintered circle of rough wooden plank, our buttocks overhanging a fetid pit, here was elegant splendour: a pit of surpassing beauty, encircled by a great golden rail. Mossy walls ran down to a limpid pool into which a lone frog gently 'plashed, barely disturbing the water-boatmen skittering across the water's mild surface, in which was reflected a trembling sky.

Installed, no doubt, for the private convenience of the Minister, should she be caught short during the long hours of her speech, it was the most beautiful sight I had yet seen in this world. It seemed nearly a shame to urinate into so perfect a pastoral picture, and it was almost with reluctance that I unbuttoned my breeches and allowed my manhood its release.

I aimed my member so as to inconvenience the Frog as little as possible. At last my Conscious made connection with my Unconscious; the Setting was Reset; Mind and Body were as One; Will became Action: I was Unified. In that transcendent moment all my senses were polished to perfection.

I could smell the sweet pollen of the Heather and the Whitethorn, and the mingled Colognes of a thousand Bachelor Farmers.

I could taste the lingering, bitter grounds of the Orphanage Coffee, and feel the grit of them lodged in the joins of my teeth.

I could see every slender, quivering stalk rising from the moist mosses lining the pit, every shivering layer of reflection upon the water, sky mingling with the pool's bottom in an exquisite balancing of visual weight, so that the frog with a powerful thrust far beneath the surface seemed to fly up through the light clouds of summer and skirt the very sun.

I could hear the murmur and sigh of the crowd like an ocean at my back, and Brünhilde DeValera's mighty voice bounding from rhetorical Peak to rhetorical Peak, ever higher.

And as this moment of Perfection began its slow decay into the past, and as the delicious frozen moment of Anticipation deliquesced into Attainment and the pent-up waters leaped forth, far forward, and fell in their glorious swoon, Brünhilde DeValera's voice rang out as from Olympus:

"I

hereby

officially

reopen...

Dev's Hole!"

A suspicion dreadful beyond words took hold of me.

I attempted to Arrest the Flow.

I may as well have attempted to block by effort of will the

course of the mighty Amazon River.

Thus the Great Curtain parted, to reveal me Urinating into Dev's Hole: into the very Source of the Sacred Spring of Irish Nationalism: the Headwater, the Holy Well, the Font of our Nation.

6.

I feel, looking back, that it would not have gone so badly against me, had I not, in my panic, turned and hosed Brünhilde De Valera with urine.

7.

They pursued me across rough ground for some considerable time.

8.

Agamemnon held my pursuers at the Gap in the Wall, as I crossed the grounds and gained the House. He had not had such vigorous exercise since running away from Fossetts' Circus to hide in our hay barn a decade before, as a pup.

Now, undaunted, he slumped in the Gap, panting at them.

Slamming the Orphanage Door behind me and turning, I came upon old Brother Thomond in the Long Corridor, beating a Small Orphan in a desultory manner.

"Ah, Jude," said Brother Thomond, on seeing me. The brown

leather of his face creaked as he smiled, to reveal the perfect, white teeth of Brother Jasper.

"A little lower, Sir, if you please," piped the Small Orphan. Brother Thomond obliged. The weakness of Brother Thomond's brittle limbs made his beatings popular with the Lads, as a rest and a relief from those of the more supple and youthful brothers.

"Yes, Jude..." he began again, "I had something I wanted to... yes... to... yes..." He nodded his head, and was distracted by straw falling past his eyes, from his tangled hair.

I moved from foot to foot, uncomfortably aware of the shouts of the approaching Mob. Agamemnon, judging by his roars, was now retreating heroically before them as they crossed the grounds toward the front door.

"'Tis the Orphanage!" I heard one cry.

"'Tis full of Orphans!" cried another.

"From Orphania!" cried a third.

"As we suspected!" called a fourth. "He is a Foreigner!"

I had a bad feeling about this. The voices were coming closer and closer. I heard the thud of Agamemnon's retreating buttocks against the door. Agamemnon stood firm at the steps, but no dog, however brave, can hold off a Mob forever.

Brother Thomond fell asleep briefly, one arm aloft above the Small Orphan.

The mob continued to discuss me on the far side of the door.

"You're thinking of Romania, and of the Romanian orphans. You're confusing the two," said a level head.

"Romanian, by God!"

"He is Romanian!"

"That man said so."

"I did not..."

"A Gypsy Bastard!"

"Kill the Gypsy Bastard!"

The Voice of Reason was lost in the hubbub, and a rock from the Rockery came in through the stained-glass window above the front door. It put a Hole in Jesus, and hit Brother Thomond in the back of the neck.

Brother Thomond awoke.

"Dismissed," he said to the Small Orphan sternly.

"Oh but Sir you hadn't finished!"

"No backchat from you, young fellow, or I shan't beat you for a week."

The Small Orphan scampered away into the darkness of the Long Corridor. Brother Thomond sighed deeply, and rubbed his neck. He turned to me.

"Ah, yes. Jude... Today is your eighteenth birthday, is it not?"

I nodded.

Brother Thomond sighed again. "I have carried a secret this long time, regarding your Birth. I feel it is only right to tell you now..."

He fell briefly asleep.

The cries of the Mob grew as they assembled, eager to enter, and destroy me. The yelps and whimpers of brave Agamemnon were growing fainter. I had but little time. I poked Brother Thomond in the clavicle with a Finger. He started awake. "What? WHAT? *WHAT?*"

Though to rush Brother Thomond was usually counter-productive, circumstances dictated that I try. I shouted, the better to penetrate both the Yellow Wax and the Fog of Years.

"You were about to tell me the Secret of my Birth, Sir."

"Ah yes. The secret..." He hesitated. "The secret of your birth... The secret I have held these many years... which was told to me by... by one of the... by Brother Feeny... who was one of the Cloughjordan Feenys... His mother was a Thornton..."

"If you could Speed It Up, Sir," I suggested, as the Mob forced open the window-catch above us. Brother Thomond obliged.

"The Secret of Your Birth..."

Outside, with a last choking yelp, Agamemnon fell silent. There was a tremendous hammering upon the old oak door.

"I'll just get that," said Brother Thomond. "I think there was a knock."

As he reached it, the door burst open with extraordinary violence, sweeping old Brother Thomond aside with a crackling of many bones in assorted sizes and throwing him backwards against the wall, where he impaled the back of his head on a coat-hook. Though he continued to speak, the rattle of his last breath rendered the Secret unintelligible. The Mob poured in.

I ran on, into the dark of the Long Corridor.

9.

I found the Master of Orphans, Brother Madrigal, in his office in the South Tower, beating an orphan in a desultory manner.

"Ah, Jude," he said. "Went the day well?"

Not wishing to burden him with the lengthy Truth, and with both time and breath in short supply, I said "Yes."

He nodded approvingly.

"May I have my Letter, Sir?" I said.

"Ah, yes... Yes, of course... The Letter..." He dismissed the small orphan, who trudged off disconsolate. Brother Madrigal turned from his desk toward the Confiscation Safe, then paused by the open window. "Who are those strange men on the Lawn, waving blazing torches?" he asked.

"I do not precisely know," I said truthfully.

He frowned.

"They followed me home," I felt moved to explain.

"And who could blame them?" said Brother Madrigal. He smiled and tousled my hair, before moving again toward the Confiscation Safe, tucked into the room's rear left corner. From the lawn far below could be heard confused cries.

Unlocking the safe, he took out the letter and walked back to face me. Behind him, outside the window, I saw flames race along the dead ivy and creepers, and vanish up into the roof timbers. "Who," he mused, looking at the envelope, "could be writing to you...?" Suddenly he started, and looked up at me. " Of course!" he said. "Jude, it is your eighteenth birthday, is it not?"

I nodded.

He sighed, the tantalising letter now dangling disregarded from his right hand. "Jude... I have carried a secret this long time, regarding your Birth. It is a secret known only to Brother Thomond and myself, and it has weighed heavy on us. I feel it is only right to tell you now... The secret of your birth..." He hesitated. "Is..."

My heart Clattered in its Cage at this Second Chance.

Brother Madrigal threw up his hands. "But where are my manners? Would you like a cup of tea first? And we must have music. Ah, music."

He pressed Play on the record player that sat at the left edge of the broad desk. The turntable bearing the Orphanage single began to rotate at forty-five revolutions per minute. The tone-arm lifted, swung out, and dropped onto the broad opening groove of the record, nearly dislodging from the needle a Ball of Dust the size and colour of a small mouse.

The blunt needle in its fuzzy ball of dust juddered through the scratched groove. Faintly, beneath the roar and crackle of its erratic passage, could be heard traces of an ancient tune.

Brother Madrigal returned to the safe and switched on the old kettle that sat atop it. Leaving my letter leaning against the kettle, he came back to his desk and sat behind it in his old black leather armchair.

Unfortunately, the rising roar of the old kettle and the roar and crackle of the record player disguised the rising roar and crackle of the flames in the dry timbers of the old tower roof.

Brother Madrigal patted the side of the Record Player affectionately. "The sound is so much warmer than from all these new digital dohickeys, don't you find? And of course you can tell it is a good-quality machine from the way, when the needle hops free of the surface of the record, it often falls back into the self-same groove it has just left, with neither loss nor repetition of much music. The Arm..." He tapped his nose and slowly closed one eye. "...Is True. One of the tips I picked up, many years ago, from old Paddy Thackery, of Thackery Electrical..."

He dug out an Italia '90 cup and a USA '94 mug from his desk, and put a teabag in each.

"Milk?"

"No, thank you," I said. The ceiling above Brother Madrigal had begun to bulge down in a manner alarming to me. The old leaded roof had undoubtedly started to collapse, and I feared my second and last link to my past would be crushed along with all my hopes.

"Very wise. Milk is fattening, and thickens the phlegm," said Brother Madrigal. "But you would like your letter, no doubt. And also... the Secret of your Birth." He arose, his head almost brushing the great Bulge in the Plaster, now big as a Bath and two foot deep.

It creaked, and settled down another inch. The white plaster was yellowing from the intense heat of the blazing roof above it. The crackle and roar of the flames was now entirely drowning out the crackle and roar of the Record Player.

"Thirty years old, that record player," said Brother Madrigal proudly, catching my glance at it. "And never had to replace the needle or the record. It came with a wonderful record, thank God. Paddy, God rest his soul, threw it in free, as a 'sweetener'. I really must turn it over one of these days," he said, lifting the gently vibrating letter from alongside the rumbling kettle whose low tones, as it neared boiling, were lost in the bellow of flame above. "Have you any experience of turning records over, Jude?"

"No sir," I replied as he returned to the desk, my letter shining white against the black of his dress. Brother Madrigal extended the letter halfway across the table. I reached out for it. The envelope, containing perhaps the secret of my origin, brushed against my fingertips, electric with potential.

At that moment, with a crash, in a bravura finale of crackle, the record came to an end. The lifting mechanism hauled the Tone Arm up off the vinyl, and returned it to its rest position as the turntable, with a sturdy click, ceased to turn.

"Curious," said Brother Madrigal, absentmindedly taking back the letter. "It is most unusual for the Crackling to continue after the Record has stopped." He stood, and moved to the Record Player. The pop and crackle of flames was by now uncommonly loud. Tilting his head from side to side, he nodded slowly. "It is in Stereo," he said. "There are a lot of Mid-Range Frequencies. That is of course where the Human Voice is strongest... I subscribed for a time to the Hi-Fi Gazette."

Behind Brother Madrigal, the Bulge in the ceiling gave a great Lurch downward. He turned, and looked up.

"Ah! There's the problem!" he said. "A Flood! Note the bulging ceiling! The water tank must have overflowed in the attic, and the subsequent Damp is causing a Crackling in the Circuits of the Record Player. Damp" (here he touched his temple twice), "is the great Enemy of the Electrical Circuit."

He was by now required to shout on account of the great noise made by the holocaust in the roof. Smoke entered the room.

"Do you smell smoke?" he enquired. I replied that I did. He nodded. "The Damp has caused a Short Circuit," he said. "Just as I suspected." He went to the corner of the room, removed a fire-ax from its glass-fronted wooden case, and strode to beneath the Bulge. "Nothing for it but to Pierce it, and relieve the pressure, or it'll have the roof down." He swung the ax up into the heart of the bulge.

A stream of liquid metal poured over him, as the pool of molten lead from the burning roof found release. Both ax and man were coated in a thick sheet of still-bright lead that swiftly thickened and set as it ran down Brother Madrigal's upstretched arm and upturned head, encasing his torso before pooling and solidifying in a thick base about his feet on the smoking carpet.

Entirely covered, he shone under the electric light, ax aloft in his right hand, my letter smoldering and silvered in his left.

I snatched the last uncovered corner of the letter from his metallic grasp, the heat-brittled triangle snapping cleanly off at the bright leaden boundary.

In that little corner of envelope nestled a small triangle of yellowed paper.

My fingers tingled with mingled dread and anticipation as they drew the scrap from its casing. Being the burnt corner of a single sheet, folded twice to form three rectangles of equal size, the scrap comprised a larger triangle of paper folded down the middle from apex to baseline, and a smaller, uncreased triangle of paper of the size and shape of its folded brother.

I regarded the small triangle.

Blank.

I turned it over.

Blank.

I unfolded and regarded the larger triangle.

Blank.

I turned it over, and read:

gents
anal
cruise.

10.

I tilted it obliquely to catch the light, the better to reread it.

gents
anal
cruise.

The secret of my origin was not entirely clear from this fragment, and the tower was beginning to collapse around me. I sighed, for I could not help but feel a certain disappointment in how my birthday had turned out.

I left Brother Madrigal's office. Behind me, the floorboards gave way beneath his lead-encased mass. I looked back, to see him vanish down through successive floors of the tower.

I ran down the stairs. A breeze cooled my face as the fires above me sucked air up the stairwell. Chaos was by now general and Orphans and Brothers sprang from every door, laughing, and speculating that Brother McGee must have once again lost control of his Woodwork Class.

The first members of the Mob began to push their way up the first flight of stairs, and, Our Lads not recognising them, fisticuffs ensued. I hesitated on the first-floor landing.

One member of the Mob broke free of the melée and exclaimed "There he is, boys!" He threw his Hat at me, and made a leap in my direction. I leapt sideways, through the nearest door, and entered Nurse's quarters.

Nurse, the most attractive woman in the Orphanage, and on whom we all had a crush, was absent at her grandson's wedding in Borris-in-Ossary. I felt it prudent to disguise myself from the Mob, and slipped into a charming blue gingham dress. Only briefly paralysed by pleasure at the scent of Nurse's perfume, I soon made my way back out through the battle, as Orphans and Farmers knocked lumps out of each other.

"Foreigners!" shouted the Farmers at the Orphans.

"Foreigners!" shouted the Orphans back, for some of the Farmers were from as far away as Cloughjordan, Ballylusky, Toomevara, Ardcrony, Lofty Bog, and even far-off South Tipperary itself, as could be told by the unusual sophistication of the stitching on the leather patches at the elbows of their tweed jackets and the richer, darker tones, redolent of the lush grasslands of the Suir valley, of the cowshit on their Wellington Boots.

"Dirty Foreign Bastards!"

"Fuck off back to Orphania!"

"Ardcrony Ballocks!"

The sophisticated farmer, who had seen The Radio Head at Punchestown, was hurled over the balcony, and his unconscious body looted of its shop-bought cigarettes by the Baby Infants.

I appeared, in Nurse's attire. The crowd parted to let me through, the Young Farmers removing their Hats as I passed. Some orphans shouted "It is Jude in a Dress!" but the unfortunate sexual ambiguity of my name served me well on this occasion and allayed the suspicions of the more doubtful farmers, who took me for an ill-favoured girl who usually wore Slacks.

At the bottom of the stairs, I found myself once again in the deserted Long Corridor.

From behind me came the confused sounds of the Mob in fierce combat with the Orphans and the Brothers Of Jesus Christ Almighty. From above me came the crack of the occasional expanding brick, a crackle of burning timber, sharp explosions of window-panes in the blazing tower.

The Mob would not rest till they found me.

My actions had led to the destruction of the Orphanage.

I had brought bitter disgrace to my family, whoever they should turn out to be.

I realised with a jolt that I would have to leave the place of my greatest happiness.

With a creak and a bang, the South Tower settled a little. Dust and smoke gushed from the ragged hole in the ceiling through which the lead-encased body of Brother Madrigal had earlier plunged. I gazed upon him, standing proudly erect on his thick metal base, holding his axe aloft, the whole of him gleaming like a freshly washed baked bean tin in the light of the setting sun that shone in through the open front door at the end of the corridor.

And by the front door, hanging from the coat-hook in his skull, his posture more alert than his old bones had been able to manage in life, was Brother Thomond. The bright yellow straw that burst up out of the neck-hole of his cassock and jutted forth from his black sleeves was stained dark red by his old, slow blood on its slow voyage to the floor.

And in the doorway itself, hung by his neck from a rope, was my old friend Agamemnon, his thick head of long golden hair fluffed up into a huge ruff by the noose, his mighty claws unsheathed, his tawny fur bristling as his dead tongue rolled from between his black lips to eclipse his fierce, yellow teeth.

What was left for me here, now?

With a splintering crash, a dull movement of air through a long moment of near-silence, and a flat, rumbling, bursting impact, the entire facade of the South Tower detached itself, unpeeled, and fell in a long roll across the lawn and down the driveway, scattering warm bricks the length of the drive.

Dislodged by the lurch and tilt of the tower, the Orphanage Record Player fell, tumbling, three stories, through the holes made by Brother Madrigal himself, and landed rightway up by his side with a smashing of innards.

The tone arm lurched onto the Record and, with a twang of elastic, the turntable began to rotate. Music sweet and pure filled the air and a sweet voice sang words I had only ever heard dimly.

"Some...

Where...

Oh...

Werther...

Aon...

Bó..."

I filled to brimming on the instant with an ineffable emotion. I felt a great... presence? No, it was an absence, an absence of? Of...

I could not name it. I wished I had someone to say goodbye to, to say goodbye to me.

It is a sad song, I think.

The record ground to a slow halt with a crunching of broken gear-teeth. I felt a soft touch on my cheek, then on the back of my hand.

I looked down to see the great ball of Dust, dislodged from the Record Player's needle during the long fall, drifting the last few inches to the ground.

I looked around me for the last time and sighed.

"There is no place like home," I said quietly to nobody, and walked out the door onto the warm bricks. The heat came up through the soles of my shoes, so that I skipped nimbly along the warm yellow bricks, till they ended.

I looked back once, to see the broken wall, the burning roof and tower.

And Agamemnon dead.

11.

The world spun me back away from the sun faster than I could walk toward it.

Night, therefore, fell.

I walked West confidently, in darkness, across the last familiar fields.

Going over a gate, the blast of wings in my face, as a barn owl braked and veered past my head in a warm blur of sensed life.

Low in the black sky, black clouds, their edges faintly glowing.

The clouds cleared to reveal a slip of a moon. All about me shimmered slowly into being, pale black and dim white in the half-moon's light, the ditch, the dreaming cattle and the smooth swell of the hills.

24

Great emotion filled me. The sensation was pleasant.

The perspiration of the moist fields condensed now in the cooling night air, forming a low haze which blocked out the stars. Small, dense clouds rose on the Western horizon, occasionally eclipsing the moon and erasing the visible world entirely. I felt content in that thick darkness, walking the invisible fields of my childhood, hearing the soft crunch of my feet on corn-stubble, or the low swish past my ankles of second-cut grass. Hearing the scattered reflection of my walking from a ditch of scraggy hazel trees to my right, or the hard, flat reflection of my walking and my breath from the concrete blocks of a silent pump-house in the corner of a field.

Sometimes I would walk softly between dreaming cattle. As I passed, some would shift their balance, with a little snort and a short step, from one diagonal to the other, the heat off them pleasant. Pleasant, too, the comforting sound of the warm wind whistling occasionally from under their tails, as the great chambers of their unsleeping stomachs digested the clean, green grass.

Sheep, more fearful of my approach, ran from me at a clatter in the least sensible direction, and often, cornered, had to double back and brush past me once again in bleating panic.

The moon, when it re-emerged, never surprised me with its revelations: it merely filled in the clean lines of my mind's-eye view.

But the dark clouds grew more frequent, and the dark grew less friendly to me the less I knew the land. Eventually I no longer knew so well the fields, the gates, the low points in the fallen walls, the gaps stopped with a single rusty strand of sagging barbed wire, easily trod down and stepped over.

I skinned a shin on a concrete feed-trough.

I nearly twisted an ankle in an unexpected patch of old rabbit holes, out in the middle of an untended field.

Minutes later, I walked into a single strand of electric fence wire, hung absurdly high. There was no charge running through it, no transformer's low buzz to warn me. It caught me in the throat and flipped my head back as my legs continued forward, so that I fell hard on my arse.

I reluctantly decided to take to the great West road.

My skin was now prickling coolly, and the animals were awake and nervous in the fields. The sky was tense with electricity, in the manner of a muscle about to kick.

I found the road by the clack of it beneath my feet. I walked West in darkness.

A curious fact, one I had often pondered, is that the full darkness of night is not Black, for Black needs a White to be Black against, and there is none in the moonless, starless night.

My darkness, then, as I walked the unseen road, was a lively thing: bursting with flashes from my excitable Retinas each time I invisibly blinked: blasts of purple and mauve, netted with intricate darker strands; jolts of what could be taken for light each time my heels hit the tarmac, sending pressure waves up my legs and torso to dissipate through my skull, firing the excitable cells of my light-hungry eyes, the sentry nerves fine-tuned to fire at anything after so long a siege in darkness.

On the narrower highway of the invisible road, I noticed a tendency in me to drift left into the grassy verge, for my right leg was stronger than my left. I tried to correct this, but over-compensated and found myself regularly encountering the right verge. With much practice, I developed the ability to match my steps exactly, so that I needed to correct my line only on the infrequent bends.

A great blast of light made me think for an instant that I had banged my head off a low branch. Indeed, it took me a moment to remember that the Visual could lie outside myself, to realise that what I had just taken for a line in my mind was a horizon, that what I had taken for a firing of cells at the back of my sockets was, in fact, a splash of lightning just beyond that horizon, outlining it, and illuminating the distant clouds from below. Or, more precisely:

the line in my mind was drawn by a distant event outside me, on the horizon, and the firing of cells was authored by the electric flash of distant lightning too far away even for its murmur to carry.

I lost, for a moment, the happy illusion that what I saw was a direct, real, thing, simply sitting there in front of me, unmediated by chemistry or biology, and I lived briefly with the uncanny knowledge that an electrochemical event had taken place in my Brain which gave me knowledge of a very recent event taking place slightly beyond the curve of the earth, but that the two events were entirely unalike in essence, scale and structure, and that my tiny inkling of what had happened was a fragment under the illusion that it held the whole.

Busy with these thoughts in my mind, I ceased to pay attention to the assorted ongoing messages of my body. It was thus I failed to notice my right foot's remark that there appeared to be no ground beneath it. Stepping heavily into the eight-inch-deep pothole marking the Tipperary side of the border, I fell headlong into County Clare.

There was an enormous blast of lightning, or so my retinas signalled. But it is possible that this was strictly an internal event of my own creation and consumption, unwitnessed and unwitnessable by any outside observer, and caused by my forehead being accelerated into the road by gravity.

Either I had received a signal indicating that a thousand gigawatts of the most violent electrical force had shredded miles of air beyond the horizon, as a torrent of electrons poured from the earth into the sky, exploding the invisible air all the way up in an instant, leaving an immense forking column of vacuum shortly to collapse along its length in a thunderclap far beyond the horizon and my hearing.

Or I had bumped my head.

And I could not tell which, and could never know, and would never know.

"This illustrates my point precisely," I thought, as I lost consciousness, with my feet in Tipperary and my head in the outside world.

12.

I awoke in a world of uniform Pinkness, and was puzzled. But I soon surmised that the cause was merely a bright light shining through my closed eyelids. I opened my eyes and lifted my head to see, sure enough, a single white lamp staring fixedly toward me. I was troubled, then, to realise that what I had been taking for the small roar of the blood pulsing in my ears was in fact a louder, throbbing growl, coming from behind the light. There was a hot, sulphurous smell in the air.

"You are alive," said a man's voice. A figure stepped from behind the light and stopped in front of me. I pondered the thick rubber soles of his black leather boots.

A motorcyclist, I thought. A motorcycle. Its headlamp. The smell of its engine.

"I am alive," I said.

Reassured, I tilted my head upward and examined the motor-cyclist by the light of the motorcycle headlamp, whose great bellow of light echoed and re-echoed off the road itself, the roadside bushes, me, and, perhaps, the very Moon.

He was a well-built bull of a man, of middling years. In his left, gauntleted, hand he held his right gauntlet. He wore large glasses, on the lenses of which could be seen the small corpses of the occasional midge or other tiny fly of the dusk or night. His motorcycle helmet was of an antique pudding-bowl design, a leather strap beneath the chin securing it, leaving the face open to the wind. The ancient helmet, its white paint chipped and scuffed, bore on the forehead a hand-painted shamrock of emerald green.

Stunned or dying moths flapped ghostly pale wings on his helmet and cheeks.

He removed the helmet and scratched his head with the fingers of his bare right hand.

His hair slowly erected itself in great tangles of grey, each tangled hair attempting to separate itself from the others, the whole mass crackling occasionally and emitting tiny sparks.

"It is the Static," he said "From this Extraordinary Electrical Storm." He pointed West, into the far heart of the dark horizon, invisible behind the glaring headlamp. A crackle of blue light at his fingertip was mirrored in a blast of light at the horizon that outshone the lamp and lit for an instant the World. "It is a great Storm, and it is coming this way."

I sighed, and shivered: I had never been so far from Home, and I felt for the first time the enormity of my exile.

Almost overwhelmed, I lowered my gaze and studied a pebble on the road in front of my nose. Grey, clean, casting a long shadow. I picked it up. Small, and easy to understand. Of the limestone used to lay the beds of the roads of Ireland. Quarried elsewhere, carried here. By truck and circumstance. A lovely rough pebble, a little scratched and chipped and dusty. There it sat, between finger and thumb. Itself, despite all.

I was comforted.

The motorcyclist spoke. I jumped to my feet with a splash, startled, and thrust the pebble in my pocket. I had forgotten his existence.

"You are out late, and it is dark. Where do you go, and what do you seek?"

I thought before I spoke. "I go, in fear and trepidation, Sir, to the Sodom of the West: Galway City."

"Galway!" He nodded slowly. Small blue sparks crackled softly in his hair. "That Republic of Possibilities, of Transformation, Danger, and Delight; that ageless merchant town, that 500-year -old City-State; the Port of Last Call for Columbus, where he prayed and provisioned before setting sail for the edge of the known universe. I am going there myself," he said, "through the heart of this storm. Do you wish for my aid on your journey?"

"Thank you, Sir," I said. He seemed a Giant of a man.

"You are standing in a Hole," he said.

I looked down. Sure enough, I stood in the mucky bottom of the pot-hole that had undone me.

"I was pondering the nature of reality," I explained.

He nodded. "It often has the same effect on me."

He extended his right hand to help me up.

Our hands met in a blast of sparks, and the sole of my right foot tingled mightily as I earthed him through the hole in the sole of my right shoe. The water sizzled and popped about my feet. Our hands leapt in each other's grasp.

"My apologies," he said, "I pick up a mighty Charge on this machine."

He gave a heave, and I stepped up and out of the pot-hole.

"Thank you, Sir."

"Think nothing of it."

He mounted the machine. I copied him, swinging my leg over the back of the beast, and settling myself astride a cosy leather seat.

"My name is Pat Sheeran," said Pat Sheeran.

He fired up the mighty engine, obliterating my reply.

"Pardon?" said Pat Sheeran.

"I've never been on a motorcycle," I said.

We turned in a tight arc till we faced the storm. "Oh it's not much different from a car, only more windy," said Pat Sheeran.

I pondered this. It did not give me as much reassurance as perhaps he had intended.

"I've never been in a car," I said.

He pondered in his turn.

"Well, it's just like riding a motorbike, only less windy," he said. "Hang on to the bar at the back."

I hung on. The world came at me at a speed I could not comprehend. My eyes snapped abruptly shut, and I sheltered in the little haven of myself.

I knew, consciously, that I was travelling at a speed unprecedented in my previous life.

Yet my mind found it impossible to believe its own senses. If I had, as a lad, ever got Riggs-Miller's mare past a canter in the old pine-grove, I would perhaps have had a personal experience of Speed, to help me comprehend what I thought I had just seen. But a Canter was as good as you got, and that only on a summer's day, when the sun had warmed her old muscles, and she was neither too close in time, nor too far, from a feed.

Still, if I had not travelled at great speed myself, I had often seen other things travelling at great speed. I decided to concentrate on recalling these memories, to see if they would assist me.

Cars passing by me.

Planes flying above my head.

Dead leaves in a storm.

This had the opposite effect to the one intended.

When I opened my eyes, I perceived myself as seated, stationary, facing into a great wind over the broad right shoulder of Pat Sheeran.

The twin roadside ditches, that seemed almost to meet in the distance, unstitched themselves and hurtled apart.

The great trees that grew here and there in the briar and hazel ditches drifted towards us at a tentative, then a worrying pace, then leaped to either side in the final second of their approach at explosive speed.

Infinite quantities of road hurled themselves forever beneath us. Dear God, what Titans could have laid such quantities of road? It seemed impossible that we could consume such distances within the narrow bounds of Ireland.

I looked left, at the nearest ditch, illuminated by the spilt light of the massive headlamp, to check it was not too close as it reeled past us, and was horrified to see that it was moving so fast it was completely out of focus. I closed my eyes, without having planned to.

"I'll stick to forty, because you've no helmet," shouted Pat Sheeran over his shoulder.

Forty miles westward, in an hour! My senses reeled. I had not travelled such a distance in a single direction in my lifetime. Would we have room to stop, before we reached the edge of our great Island?

13.

"I was at the Fianna Fáil hat-flinging rally," shouted Pat Sheeran.

I opened one eye. "Really?"

"Yes. Some young radical hosed the minister with Piss."

I opened the other eye. "Really?"

"Yes. I could have killed the little bastard," said Pat Sheeran.

A fly of the night flew down my throat at forty miles an hour and I spent some time coughing him back up again.

"Really?" I said eventually.

"Yes. I'd a meeting scheduled with the Minister for after the Speeches, but she cancelled everything."

"You didn't recognise the Pisser?" I asked. Pat Sheeran turned and looked at me.

"Little bastard," said Pat Sheeran, and I pondered the consequences of leaping from a motorcycle at nearly the legal speed limit. I was held back by my strong intuition that there was likely to be a transfer of energies not to my benefit. Pat Sheeran turned his attentions back to the road. "No, I was too far back, and my view was obscured by the Mosh-Pit." I relaxed a fraction. He continued, "I would have had a better view if I'd arrived on time and taken my VIP seat, but I was delayed."

"And how was that?" I asked, greatly relieved to be steering the conversation away from myself.

"I had a vital letter to deliver to the local Orphanage," he said. "As a favour to..." He trailed off as we cornered.

My heart rose and fell at the one time: a sickly feeling.

"It made me late. The speeches had started, and I could not make my way to my seat upon the stage. Or I'd have caught and killed the little bastard. For apparently the Radical Pisser," he turned and glared, "sat in my very chair."

"A bastard indeed," I said, "Yes." I ached to ask of the Letter he had delivered. As a favour to whom? And why could it not be trusted to the post?

But did he know that the Radical Pisser and the Letter's Addressee were the self-same Orphan? If so, to reveal it was my Letter was to unleash his wrath, and seal my doom. There is no hiding place on a motorbike. I proceeded cautiously.

"Did you know it was the same Jude, to whom you were deliv-ering the letter, that sat in your seat, pissed upon the Minister, and destroyed your careful plans?"

"What!" said Pat Sheeran. "That little bastard was Jude?" He turned and stared at me.

No, he had not known. That was good. Unfortunately, my careful questioning had let slip the connection. That was bad. I sighed. Best to change the subject, for now. I would bide my time. "And for what reason were you due to meet the Minister?"

"I wanted her to help me produce my Device. I was also hoping to give her one."

"I beg your pardon?" I said, for the wind was loud in my ears, and I thought I had perhaps misheard.

"In the Technological Future," said Pat Sheeran, with the Zeal of the Convert, "we will all carry a Small European Phone, a more expensive yet less functional Small American Phone for travelling in America, a Paging device, a Shirt-Pocket Computer, a Digital Record Player, a Computerised Health Monitor, an Electronic

Notepad with Cyber-Pencil, a Personal Bar-Code Reader, a Handy Digital Watch-cum-Global Positioning System, an All-Purpose Remote Control... and one of These..."

To my intense distress, he took his left hand off the steering-bar of the motor-cycle, and rummaged in his capacious pockets.

With a "Hah!" he bore aloft a strange Device.

"What is it?"

"It is," said Pat Sheeran, "The Thirteenth Device."

I made some rapid mental calculations. "You are counting the Electronic Notepad and Cyber Pencil as two devices?" I said.

"Yes, and also the Handy Digital Watch-cum-Global Positioning System," said Pat Sheeran. "Naturally the white heat of Technology will meld all these vital devices, combining them until we have only to carry perhaps seven or eight machines. But mine is set to be the most Vital of all... And I've over a hundred million dollars of Venture Capital behind me to ensure it is so."

"Fair play to you," I said. "What is it?"

"Well, mostly, inside this casing - and elsewhere, on gigantic Servers - and spread throughout the globe in tiny self-sufficient sub-routines, it is... a Program."

"Ah! A Program!" I said, feeling the answer retreat even as I advanced the question. "What is it?"

"It is a revolutionary evolutionary algorithm," said Pat Sheeran.

My heart did not rise. "What," I said, "is it?"

He took another run at it. "It is a delivery system for the most valuable product of all. A product which adds value to all other products. A product without which no product is of value to you."

"A Product. And what," I asked, "...is," and my voice seemed a whisper in my own ears, so tired was I by now after this long night, "...it?"

"Wisdom," said Pat Sheeran. "The Lost Product. For though the technology of the day connects every Machine to every other

Machine, puts all Data within reach of every searching hand, makes every answer but a question away, yet that is not Wisdom. That is mere Information. For who can define the Problem, who can phrase the Question, in such a way as to elicit the perfect Answer from all possible Answers?"

"Not I," I said quietly. "Not I."

"You are familiar with the Irish Legends?"

"Yes," I said. "Roy Keane, Gay Byrne and Dana."

"I was thinking of older Legends than that."

"Jack Charlton?" I essayed tentatively.

"No," said Pat Sheeran.

"You hold his Yorkshire roots against him," I said.

"Perhaps it is best if I jog your memory," said Pat Sheeran. "The Fir Bolg, or bellymen, ruled Ireland. The Tuatha de Danaan, or people of the Goddess Dana…"

I had known I was right, and chafed now at the injustice of his correction.

"… a more cultured, skilled and civilized people, came to Ireland and raped, slaughtered and enslaved the uncivilized Fir Bolg. Then the noble Milesians, the exquisitely cultured and civilized descendants of Milesius of Spain, came to Ireland and raped, slaughtered and enslaved the uncivilized Tuatha de Danaan and Fir Bolg… We are up to three thousand years ago now…"

We hit an owl. My attention wandered briefly. When my attention returned, it found Pat Sheeran still speaking.

"Finn MacCumhail had all the characteristics of a great warrior, bar two: poetry, and wisdom. And so he was sent to live with an old poet on the banks of the Boyne River. And the old poet taught him the trick of poetry. But the poet had been trying for seven years to catch the bradán feasach, or Salmon of Knowledge: for the first person to taste the Salmon of Knowledge would, in an instant, know all the world's wisdom. So the poet asked Finn MacCumhail to catch and cook the bradán feasach for him in payment, but not to taste it. And Finn caught it, with his mighty warrior's hunting skills, and cooked it. But turning it over in the fire, he burnt his thumb on the hot fish, and he sucked his thumb, and tasted the Salmon of Knowledge, and knew in an instant all the world's wisdom. And from that day on, if he ever had a problem, all he had to do was suck his thumb."

He had stopped.

"That would be before my time," I said apologetically.

Pat Sheeran nodded. "What we need today is a Salmon of Knowledge. Our Algorithm knows where you are, thanks to the Global Positioning System. It knows who you are, thanks to the information you provided when you set up your account. And it knows what your Problem is likely to be, based on your Personality Profile, your Health Status, the Weather or Traffic conditions at your location, the World News, the Local News, and a thousand other variables, including a degree of Randomness which you are also free to vary. You may ask it for wisdom, at moments of crisis, at the touch of a button. Or you may set it to volunteer Wisdom to you as the Algorithm sees fit. Each time, the sea of information by which you are surrounded is desalinated, distilled, filtered into a drop of Wisdom to wet your lips, and to slake your thirst. Here." He passed it back to me.

I examined it. The unbroken sleek silver curves of the case appealed to me greatly. "It is beautiful," I said.

"Yes," said Pat Sheeran, "It is modelled on Brancusi's *Fish*, a sculpture I particularly admire. We improved it slightly, giving it a gently textured finish for better grip."

I stroked the curves of the Device. "It weighs so little..."

"Its casing is made from Titanium. It is extraordinarily light for its strength."

"The feel of it in the hand is wonderful..." I could not help but stroke its burnished sides, on which was embossed the most delicate rippling pattern. I examined it as well as I could by the leaping light of the headlamp, by the silvery light of the occasional moon. Like the soft, silver scales of a salmon's belly seen suddenly through water... I felt a curious desire, which I could not recall feeling before.

I examined the Device.

I examined the Desire.

The two were related. With a start, I realised that what I desired was the Device. I wanted something I had never wanted before: to Possess an Object.

"It is designed by Jonathan Ives," said Pat Sheeran. "An Englishman who more usually works for the Apple Corporation, in America."

"Do many yet have this fine device?" I said.

"Almost nobody," said Pat Sheeran. "Which is entirely to be expected at this early stage, and is fully in line with the Business Plan. At the moment the unit cost is ten thousand US dollars, though obviously the cost will drop as we ramp up volume production. Ten thousand dollars has proved a difficult price point. Thus, in order to build market share, we are giving them away free. Our future customer base is projected to own the other Twelve major devices by next year. Unfortunately, our trial-period customers do not yet own them. Thus these prototypes must also remotely monitor your health, contain a Global Positioning System transponder etc in order to function, which pushes up the cost. There will be huge savings when in the digitally integrated future, early next year, we can take our positional, health, traffic, purchasing and mood information from the other devices. It will also reduce the size and weight of the product considerably. In short, owning a Salmon of Knowledge will soon make," he cleared his throat, "All the Sense in the World™."

"Pardon?" I said. "I didn't catch the last bit."

"Trademark... We registered it as our Trademark. Our lawyers have advised me to indicate, each time I use it, that we own it."

"You own All the Sense in the World?"

"Trademark... Yes. Just as, for example, the Callaway Golf Company owns Enjoy the Game™..."

As we discussed the Salmon of Knowledge, the landscape changed slowly to stone.

14.

Later, the conversation grew more philosophical.

He shrugged. "The person you see is not Me."

I looked carefully at the back of his head. "You certainly bear a most striking resemblance to yourself," I said.

"The Me you see," said he, "Is a construction in your head. You know nothing of my past, have no access to my interior life, must take it on trust that I do not mislead you with my present words and deeds..."

"Fill me in," I urged, "That I may know you better. That we may be friends to each other."

"Where to begin?" he sighed, as a grove of trees flicked past.

"The Past," I suggested, as a village stuttered by. How I hoped he would reveal something of my Origins without my having to reveal my identity to him and risk destruction. A playground and a graveyard passed in two breaths as he pondered.

"As a child, I thought of the world as containing Good and Evil," he said. "I wished to be Good in a Good world, I wished not to be Evil in an Evil world. This view of the world made me sad much of the time, and guilty for the rest...

"As a young man, I thought of the world as containing Right and Left. I wished to be Left in a Left world, I wished not to be Right in a Right world. This view of the world made me sad much of the time, and angry for the rest...

"I discovered the religions of the East, and I wished to integrate my Yin and Yang in a Yin-Yang world. This left me feeling confused a lot of the time, though, in compensation, I did levitate twice.

"But all of them seemed to involve dualities: Good and Bad, by different names. In the West, Good fights Bad in endless battle. In the East, Good and Bad are the opposite faces of an endlessly rotating unity.

"All these philosophies exhausted my heart. All seemed to come from some other world to the one I knew. None had room for my Rage, my Hunger, my Lust. When I was Good, and Left, and One, I still lived in a world that seemed Bad, and Right, and Many. I became banjaxed by anger and grief.

"But meanwhile, Ireland had changed around me. It had, without my noticing, abandoned my childhood Religion, and with it Good and Evil. It had tried, and abandoned, the Struggle for Social Justice, and with it Left and Right. It had entirely sidestepped the Genius of the East, ignoring five thousand years of subtle discourse as though it had never happened. And it had adopted a philosophy, or secular Religion, that required nobody to change anything about themselves at all. A Religion with no God, an Ideology that contained no Dualities, and a Philosophy with no Teachings: High Capitalism. And I gave myself to it. And I was free.

"As a Free Economic Agent, I discovered that in truth I did not want to save the Third World, for I was not prepared to pay for it. All my anger and guilt melted away. As an economic agent, I discovered what I believed in, and it made more sense than all my old theories. I believed in Food. I believed in Wine. I believed in Books. I believed in the comfort of a Warm House and a Big Bed. I believed in the company of beautiful women, in sharing with them, in buying for them, Food, and Wine, and Books. In this religion at last I recognised myself accepted, not judged, for my Anger, my Hunger, my Lust.

"At Nimmo's Restaurant, by the Spanish Arch in Galway City, as I paid for a wonderful dinner with my credit card, all the while looking into my beloved's eyes, I was converted to Reality, to the Modern World, to the New Ireland. I bowed to the Western Zen that accepts the illusion of Money, that weightless thing, that spirit that is everywhere and nowhere, that nothing in everything. The Holy Spirit of Capitalism.

"And I realised that the West is the Yin to the Yang of the East: That by running to Kyoto and Tibet I was not approaching but fleeing the truth. I looked about me. I saw that my Lemon Meringue Pie with Fresh Cream was four Irish pounds and ninety-nine Irish pence, its price clear upon the bill, and I did not ration my love. I loved the Pie, and the Bill, and the Price. I accepted all things. And in that moment I was enlightened."

The trees and fields and the dark houses passed us by in what I thought of now as silence, having grown so accustomed to the noise of motorbike and wind. "Tell me of the Present, and the Future," I said. Though the Past had yielded no treasure, I hoped a hint might yet emerge of how he came to be delivering me a Letter on my Birthday. Could he possibly be...? No. No? No.

"In the Present, I am simply here," he shrugged. "As to the Future, the Future which seems so inevitable in hindsight, the Future we create daily through our choices and their interaction with the choices of others: I believe that single Future to be an illusion."

"How so?" I said, interested, for I thought of myself as moving into the future, and would have to rethink my plans if there was no such thing.

"The Future is an illusion because, at the most fundamental level, Choice is an illusion. I am a believer in the theory, popular among physicists, that every time there is a Choice, the universe splits: both choices come to pass, but in now-separate universes. And so on, and on, with every choice of every particle, every atom, every molecule, every cell, every being, coming into being. In this universe of universes, everything happens, and every combination of things happens. Our universe is a mote of dust in an ever-growing dust-storm of possibilities, but each mote of dust in that storm is generating its own dust-storm of possibilities every instant, the motes of which in turn... But you get the general impression. Indeed, to think of ourselves as single selves, and our universe as a single universe, is to be blinded, by the limitations of our senses and our consciousness, to the infinite-faceted truth: that we are infinite in a universe of universes that are each infinitely infinite..."

"An intriguingly intricate view of the world," I said, wriggling my right foot. The pebble I had put in my pocket had just cut through my pocket's frayed bottom and slid down my trouser-leg into my shoe.

Pat Sheeran nodded. "And it is astonishing how little practical difference it makes," he said. "All my other lives are as inaccessible to me as if they did not exist at all. No doubt in other universes I am a beggar, a revolutionary, an academic, an accountant; a drinker, a thinker, a writer of books; I lose a freckle, gain a mole, shade off into men nothing like me at all; I have sons, fire guns, live forever, die too young. Whenever any particle in this universe changes state, I am split and travel in both directions, multiplied. But here I am, suffering the illusion of unity in this endlessly bifurcating moment.

"Yet, sometimes, I wave my arms for the joy of creating a spray of universes."

I said, startled at the implications, "Though it may make no practical difference, the implications are nonetheless startling."

"Indeed," said Pat Sheeran. "I had immediately to file all the Fiction on my shelves under Non-Fiction. For it is an unavoidable corollary of this theory, that Fiction is impossible. For all novels are true histories of worlds as real as ours, but which we cannot see. All stories are possible, all histories have happened. I, billion-bodied, live a trillion lives every quantum instant. Those trillion lives branch out, a quintillion times a second, as every particle in every atom in each mote of dust on land, in sea, and sky, and space, and star, flickering in and out of being in the void, hesitates, and decides its next state. All tragedies, all triumphs, are mine, are yours."

"It is a curious and difficult thing, to think that all is possible. No, probable. No, certain," I said, attempting to grasp the largeness of the thought. "That nothing is improbable."

"It is a comforting thought, some nights, to this version of me, now," said Pat Sheeran, and we roared on.

How soon we grow accustomed to the impossible. On the back of the motorbike, sheltered from the wind by the broad back of Pat Sheeran, I was at length lulled to sleep by the roar of the uncountable explosions per second in the pistons of the massive engine beneath me, by the bellow of the hot gases from the fat exhaust pipe, by the infinite generation of new universes each instant as we roared through space, as we bellowed through time, in a cascading explosion of exploding, cascading universes.

GALWAY

15.

I awoke on the very crest of fabled Prospect Hill in Galway City, to see a bolt of lightning split the sky. Its white flash outlined a dark cloud of bats against the soaring tower of Galway's greatest building, the Car-Park of the Roaches. We plunged down Prospect Hill towards the heart of the city, towards Eyre Square.

A Guard emerged from a public house and stepped into the road in front of us.

"The implacable forces of Order!" cried Pat Sheeran over his shoulder. "I accept the Guard's good intentions. I accept my own rebellion against his intentions. Leap off the bike, and be sure your feet are running before they hit the ground. This is the heart of Galway on a Saturday Night. You must embrace it, and I must flee."

He slowed the motorcycle as we approached the Guard.

I leapt off, and began running, as he had instructed, in mid-air. And found the transition to ground effortless.

I covered half of Eyre Square at a sprint, the next quarter of Eyre Square at a trot. I ambled through an eighth of Eyre Square, and I drifted to a halt with only a sixteenth of Eyre Square ahead of me.

I looked back over my shoulder. The Guard was trying to block a wraith upon a shadow. Pat Sheeran in his black leathers and his motorcycle in its black paint seemed to soak up the invisibly fast flicker of the electric street lights, seemed to shimmer in and out of existence. He had slowed down rather than speeded up, cut his engine and drifted. He had obscured his white helmet with one huge, dark gauntlet. Giving back no light, it was hard to tell if Pat, or his bike, were really there at all.

The Guard's firm, blocking hand–gesture grew tentative, apologetic, embarrassed… Unsure now, he almost groped the air around him, pulled his hands back, looked about self-consciously, to see was he being observed flapping at the air. He caught my eye and stared at me with a bewildered expression. A shadow drifted by him on the other side. An engine roared. He turned to see Nothing. It disappeared around the corner of the Square. The Guard scowled, and took a step toward me.

The weight of my black bag reminded me of Pat Sheeran's gift. I took out the Salmon of Knowledge. Now would be a fine time for a drop of Wisdom. But the Salmon lay still in my palms, and did not speak. I was reassured. Evidently I had enough Wisdom, and needed no more. I put it back in my bag.

A distant church bell chimed the hour of two a.m. Between the first stroke and the second, the nightclubs of Galway disgorged their contents onto the streets. A crowd milled about me, about the Guard: we were lost to each other. I was spun around, and around. A woman took me by the elbow, a man took a swing at me, and I spun and ducked and waltzed my way to the edge of the crowd.

There, stunned, I beheld a tremendous transparent building, lit from within with golden light. Its splendour dominated the West side of the Square.

A building so vast and beautiful could only be a Temple; and sure enough, through its walls of glass, I saw an enormous congregation facing a long low altar behind which a priesthood seemed busy at their rituals.

Outside it, young people milled about, many of them on their knees on the pavement, their heads bowed thoughtfully over what appeared to be modest food offerings.

Glowing a fiery red above its teeming entrance was the Word: "SUPERMACS". As though hypnotised, I found myself drawn inside.

And then I saw her.

A vision far ahead of me, wreathed in mist from her chip-pan: the most beautiful girl in the world. And I realised this was a Chip Shop the size of Killaloe Cathedral. And I realised I was in Love.

I looked upon her Surface, and imagined her Depths. And the wild beating of my heart caused my blood to surge faster through the narrow channels of my body, so that the roar of blood in my ears deafened me, and my sight dimmed, and I grew faint.

I shall not describe her face, for its glory lay not in its geometry, nor its proportion, nor its symmetry. No. No description would convey the relevant information.

Her body was muffled under a uniform designed, by its look, for neither fashion nor comfort. Yet the way in which she inhabited her body, the way in which she deployed her face, the colour and heat of the spark of life in her illuminated the temple of her flesh…

In a trance, I walked towards her, and bumped into a counter. Various people tried to step in front of me, poking my chest.

"A!"

"U!" they shouted.

"Q!"

I had no time for their riddles. I knocked them carefully aside, vaulted the counter, and walked to her.

"My name is Jude," I said. "I have fallen deeply in love with you at first sight."

In a voice like the whisper of silk against an angel's wing, she said, "You're taking the piss, right?"

I reassured her that I was in earnest.

"Are we on television?" she replied.

"Not to my knowledge," I said.

A selection of anxious young men in grease-spattered uniforms ceased to Feed the Hungry, and gathered in the aisle near us. They engaged in fierce debate, in expletive-flecked undertones. Some then went back, to quell unrest among the neglected masses. At length, the eldest youth pushed forward the youngest.

The young man approached me, speckled with spots, his hair encased in a curious net.

"Please sir, please could you return to the other side of the counter, sir. Please. Sir." I looked down at him, greatly moved. No one had ever spoken to me with such politeness and evident respect before. This young man was obviously deeply spiritual, to speak with such humility to a poor Tipperary Orphan such as I. A fellow far along the path to enlightenment, or indeed a high priest of some sort. Though he seemed young for such a role, I knew that in certain faiths the greatest spiritual leaders were often trained from birth. Like the Dalai Lama in Buddhism, and also the Panchen Lama, of whom I had read.

"Are you a Lama?" I asked him. He very slowly backed away from me without replying. No doubt his humility forbade him from boasting of his high spiritual status. Ah well. I returned to my conversation with the most beautiful woman I had ever seen.

Next thing I knew, my arms were pinned behind my back and I was being hurled over the counter by uniformed Guardians of the Peace.

"Drunk. Or high. He thought I was a sheep," the polite young man was telling them.

"Lama! Lama!" I appealed to him, as I was hustled out the door.

"Llama, sheep, whatever," said the young man. A curious crowd gathered around me.

"I love her," I tried to explain.

"Sheep shagger," shouted someone. The crowd began to chant, "Sheep shagger". Someone threw a curried chip. My attempts at explanation seemed only to make matters worse. The crowd closed in. I racked my mind for a clever plan.

I ran...

16.

"Sheep shagger! Sheep shagger!" roared the crowd, as they pursued me down Shop Street.

The crowd, as is the way of large, running, roaring crowds, drew a crowd of its own from the after-hours drinkers, musicians and bar-staff in the pubs and clubs and alleys we passed. From The Imperial, from Garavans, from both Lower and Upper Abbeygate Street, from the Snug and Church Lane and Taaffes they came pouring. Many of these inebriated onlookers joined unsteadily in the chase. Unsure of whom it was they were chasing, many of them fought the front-runners of the chasing pack.

I made good use of this confusion to increase my lead, but soon I was slowed by a stitch in my side and the stone in my shoe. Limping, in agony, with my pursuers so close I could smell their porter breath over my shoulder, I threw myself through a narrow church gate, in search of Sanctuary.

The crowd crashed to a halt against the railings behind me. Strong men held the gateposts and bulged every sinew to stop the crush pushing them through the open gate. Not a soul followed me.

"'Tis Saint Nicholas's Collegiate Church!" one cried. "He will be eaten by Protestants!"

I limped into the great Church. Several old ladies and an even older gentleman looked up at me, startled. The old gentleman approached me, with great caution.

Trying to remove the stone from inside the heel of my shoe, I absentmindedly extended my right hand under my raised left knee, to shake his hand. He raised his knee and did likewise, with a great creaking of bones.

"You are a Mason!" he exclaimed with pleasure, standing on one leg.

Me, a mason? It was true I had built a short stretch of the Orphanage Wall, after block-laying instruction from Brother O'Driscoll, but to call me a mason seemed excessive flattery. The wall had fallen in the first high wind, leaving a Gap, and crushing a number of Orphans.

"Why, you are a gift sent from Heaven," said an old lady. "We were just saying we needed a young man to be Warden of Saint Nicholas's now that Ramsey has retired. But there are no God-fearing young Church of Ireland men in this parish any more, for we have stopped Breeding."

Warden...

"What would my duties be?" I asked, interested.

"Well, to Ward," said a second lady.

"And to Save Electricity," said a third. "And if you could play the Bells now and then..."

"What is your name, young man?" asked the old man, dashing my hopes on the instant. Oh curse the day the Brothers of Jesus Christ Almighty christened me after the Patron Saint of Hopeless Causes! My Catholicism revealed, I would be denied Wardenship and Sanctuary and be cast out, to be torn limb from limb by my fellow Catholics in an orgy of both violence and irony. "And I suppose," he mused, "technically, we should also ask for a Curriculum Vitae, a Tax Clearance Certificate, Credit History and two references from senior figures in the Church of Ireland community."

My dreams lay blasted. Not a one of these had I. I searched

my mind for a Reference from a senior figure in the Church of Ireland.

Lost in thought, I put down my left foot. Unfortunately, the stone had been stood on end, sharp point up, by my poking. It pierced my heel as I placed all my weight on it.

I spoke in tongues, put my head between my knees, lifted the foot, lost my balance, and recovered it by grabbing the old man, through his loose tweed, by the testicle, and slowly lowering my forehead to the cold stone.

I let go his testicle, raised my head, and hopped.

"Well, well, well," said the old man. "A Mason of so high a rank, and so young! You were modest earlier, with your greeting of the Fourth Rank. We may skip the formalities." He bowed low. With a creak and a groan, he removed his right shoe and tweaked, with his toes, through the cotton of his shirt, his left nipple, before handing me the keys to Church, Sacristy, and Bell Tower. He put on his shoe.

They bade me goodnight, and left. I made my way up the Bell Tower and explored the store cupboards.

The contents were sparse, but sufficient for comfort. Tools, glue, oilcans, polish, an old pillow used to muffle the bells...

I lay on the pillow and sniffed the glue nostalgically, for it reminded me of my happy childhood in the Orphanage. I drifted off to sleep, and dreamt I was a camel.

When the sun woke me next morning, I discovered that the glue had stuck my Pillow firmly to my back. It would not budge. I pulled my clothes on over it. This gave me a somewhat unusual appearance. Sighing, I brushed my teeth with my Travel Toothbrush, in the sunny Bell-tower window.

Then, of a sudden, I spied, far below me on Shop Street, The Most Beautiful Girl In The World. My heart clattered like a stick along railings.

"It is I, Jude, your Admirer!" I cried, my speech somewhat impeded by toothpaste.

She looked up, and saw me.

I cannot account for what followed, unless it were that I did not look my best, hunchbacked as I was, in a Bell Tower, and frothing at the mouth.

She turned pale, her knees gave way, and she toppled slowly to the pavement.

My love lay there, unmoving.

17.

Dropping my toothbrush, I leapt down the twisting wooden stairs of the Bell Tower. Tripping on the last landing, I tumbled the final fifty feet. Luckily, I was protected from lasting damage by the Pillow glued to my back, and by my Head, which between them absorbed the majority of the impacts.

Gaining the street, I hobbled to my unconscious Beloved's side, in the shadow of Eason's the News-Agents. I carried her limp form back to safety, to the Bell Tower of Saint Nicholas, a place I had already come to think of as home. I lowered her gently to the floor.

I gazed down upon her.

Her radiant face.

Her generous frontage. She no longer wore her uniform but rather a child's Tea Shirt sprinkled with glitter.

Her eyelids flickered, and opened. "I," she said in a voice like honey flowing from a jug of gold, "will never drink Red Bull and vodka again."

Then her eyes focused, and she leaped a Foot. My appearance had not been improved by my fall. In addition to my hump and my frothing at the mouth, I had cricked my neck and was now forced to look at her entirely sideways. I abandoned my plan to play it Cool.

"I love you!" I cried, perhaps too energetically, through the pain and toothpaste.

"Yuk!" she replied. She declined my offer of assistance, preferring to remove the toothpaste from her hair herself as I continued.

"I am poor, but honest. Could you find it in your heart to love me?"

She searched her heart, as she backed toward the door. At the top of the stairs she found her answer: "No!"

And, overcome no doubt by womanly emotion, she sprinted downstairs in high heels, her tiny skirt inverted by the rushing wind, her skin-tight top failing to restrain her magnificent Jiggling.

Distraught, I called from the Tower as she reappeared in the Church grounds below me, "Is there not a task I could perform, to change your mind and win your heart?"

"Yeah, sure!" she called up as she ran, and my heart leapt like a salmon. "Get plastic surgery to look like Leonardo DiCaprio. And make a million more on..."

And with that tantalising promise she was gone...

The first part of her request was clear, though I puzzled over the second one briefly. A million more on what? But of course! A million more on top of what I had already!

I was ecstatic, transformed. The woman I loved had set me a task.

I gazed, sideways, from my tower, at the glorious new day.
She loved me!

18.

The lady at the till in Eason's the News-Agents directed me to a number of magazines in a range of shades of pink.

Thus commenced the Research for my Quest.

Mr. DiCaprio appeared to be a well-known film actor with an astonishingly small nose. I was unfamiliar with his *oeuvre*. I memorised his curious features, and read the captions and surrounding text. He had starred in a film about a boat. And yet his position in the cultural Pantheon did not seem entirely assured. He was In according to some magazines, yet he was Out according to more, while others believed his hairline to be in recession. A small minority compared him unfavourably to a rodent, native to North America, called the Chip-Monk.

I sighed. It would take a great deal of reconstructive surgery to fashion my face into his. Besides which, I had not the money to pay for such a reshaping.

I slipped a free Full-Colour Pop Sticker of Mr. DiCaprio into my pocket. Yes, my priority would have to be the earning of a million pounds. I left Eason's the News-Agents, filled with a stern resolve.

19.

Down Shop Street I limped, asking in each Premises for a Job. It would be hard, I knew, earning a Million. How hard I was not entirely sure, for I had never found it necessary to count past Five Hundred and One. But hard it would certainly be.

Five hours later, I found myself on the fringes of the City. Every business in Galway had Refused me work. My feet were raw and blistered, and my throat ruined from Asking. My cricked neck had stiffened further, and I had found it impossible to remove the pillow from my back. I sighed, with difficulty: half a pint of glue from the night before still blocked my nostrils completely. I breathed laboriously through my mouth. Mild, ongoing fume intoxication, via the sinuses, caused my hands and facial muscles to twitch erratically.

At this very moment, dangerously close to the brink of despair, I looked up, sideways, and I beheld the most magnificent Shed I had ever seen, its galvanised roof a-glitter in the sun. Above its door a single word: NORTEL. The immense shed hummed with the vibration and sound of machinery. The car park surrounding it was filled with motor cars, many of them taxed and insured. The very air was alive with the aroma of gainful employment. Here in this Shed alone, I thought, there must be more Jobs than in all Tipperary.

I felt like Moses, of the Bible, gazing upon the Promised Land.

Tired, footsore, I entered. Ahead of me was a silver Chair, with the wheels of a Chariot, and little footrests. Frowning people rushed about, shouting.

"Is he here yet?"

"He's delayed!"

"Is everything ready for the demonstration?"

As if in a dream, I walked toward the chair. I slumped into it. I put my feet up, and relaxed. A pleasant, warm sensation between my shoulders…

Harsh, familiar fumes lulled me to sleep.

"Who's that in the chair? Get out of the chair!" came a shout.

I woke, panicked and tried to rise. Disaster! The glue had warmed, soaked through my shirt, and stuck my hump to the chair. Snarling Nortel employees approached me. I flailed wildly, striking the chair's many buttons. Machinery whined to life beneath my seat, and the wheelèd Chair zoomed forward, out the doors of Nortel, across the car park, through a shrubbery, accelerating toward the forbidding tinted glass doors of a low-slung building marked WESTCOM.

The doors whooshed open before me automatically, and I hurtled past a gigantic receptionist, along an enormous corridor, past a wide-eyed child, through a vast mahogany door, to Crash finally into an immense Desk.

A large man looked down at me. I looked up at him, my head sideways, my back bent, the morning's toothpaste crusted at the corner of my mouth.

"Why, Professor Stephen Hawking!" he cried. "I'm honoured!"

I tried to speak, but my throat had seized up from rawness and the glue-fumes.

He continued, "I guess people say this all the time, but you look bigger in real life than on Television." He shook his head. "What can I, as President of Westcom, do for you?"

I noticed a small, peculiar typewriter bolted to the arm of my Wheelèd Chair, and pondered a moment. No, I was too exhausted to explain his error. I typed my simple request. A synthetic Computer Voice instantly spoke, startling me. "I...WANT... A... JOB... SIR," it said.

"A job!" cried the American. "For Professor Stephen Hawking? The Genius of our Age? The New Einstein? Why, of course! By God, this'll put one up Nortel!"

I thanked him.

"Call me Barney," said the huge President of Westcom. "Barney O'Reilly Fitzpatrick McGee. Born and bred in Orange County, California, but my folks are originally from a little town called Kórqûe, in the County of Münster. I like to think that, though an American, I am more Irish Than The Irish Themselves." He winked at me. "I'll try not to hold your being a Brit against you." And he shook my limp hand with a great Grinding of my Small Bones. His face became very serious. As, indeed, did mine. "Steven, you are a man of Wisdom. I would be honoured if you would be Westcom's Consultant on a Major Project."

I nodded, insofar as I could, my head being sideways, my acceptance.

"Pardon?"

54

"Yes," I typed. YES, said the computer voice. "I accept." I ACCEPT, said the computer voice.

"Great! It's a fascinating project. I think you'll enjoy it..." He smiled. "Very soon, I will show you something very few men have ever seen." And, in a gesture which brought back happy memories of the Orphanage Dances, he put his hand between his legs under the great Desk. "But first," said Barney O'Reilly Fitzpatrick McGee, pausing, "In the interests of protecting Shareholder Value... in the interests of Transparency... there will have to be... oh, it is the merest formality!..."

He Pulled a hidden Handle.

"...An Interview..."

The entire Office began to sink, desk and all, down a gigantic liftshaft.

We descended into darkness.

20.

We emerged into light.

The Office slowed to a halt on some kind of vast spot-lit platform. On the platform was a huge, ring-shaped banqueting table, draped in golden cloth. A single gap broke the ring. The mahogany desk slotted silently into the gap, completing the circle. Silent servants swiftly threw a gold cloth over the bare desktop and laid our places.

From around the ring, a dozen seated men in suits hailed us. "Barney, we nearly started without you."

I blinked about me: I sensed a vast space beyond the lit stage, but was dazzled by the spotlights.

He whispered to me, "Just a group of friends, fellow golfers, humble servants – Servants! - of Global Capital, meeting up for lunch, to celebrate… well," he broke off. "Sorry guys, I was delayed. Meet the Einstein of the Age: Professor Stephen Hawking."

They gasped, then spoke.

"Oh man, I loved you in Star Trek,"

"You were great in The Simpsons,"

"My first wife is still reading your book."

"Thank you," I typed, assuming these to be compliments. "THANK… YOU…"

"I'm Bill Gates, the software multi-billionaire," said a pale, bespectacled man called Bill Gates, and all the others laughed.

"Why of course he knows who *we* are!" said one.

Two suited men leaned closer to me.

"Bill's a little weird?" whispered the tall pale man.

"Set up his own company? With his own money?" whispered the short pale man, and his eyeballs rolled up in their sockets.

Bill Gates looked over at them, with a look which I could not interpret.

Both men coughed.

Barney filled the awkward silence. "Professor Hawking is interested in a consultancy role on Westcom's new project. Obviously, before giving him the Shareholders' money, there should be a rigorous interview… For we have a Sacred Trust: to protect Shareholder Value…" All bowed their heads briefly. Some mumbled prayers. "And by happy coincidence, looking around me, I see that all of Westcom's Independent Directors happen to be here today… Ted, Fred, Ned…"

A selection of suited men jerked erect from their prayers.

"Why so we are!"

"Golly, that's true."

"Who'd a thought?"

My mind was abuzz with thinking and glue fumes. An interview… I recalled that the Lads had sometimes been sent for interviews, for the practice, in all the mighty businesses of Town, both Shoe-shop and Chip-shop. The Lads had boasted of their prowess later, while emptying their pockets of leather Shoes, and emptying the Shoes of warm Chips... I searched my mind for more memories. Preparation, yes preparation had been considered crucial. Money! They had asked for money, to give the illusion of Interest and Enthusiasm.

"Is there a wage? I typed. "IS THERE A WAGE."

The men laughed. "I like his style!" "No bullshit." "A swift mind."

"So what kind of money were you thinking?" asked Barney.

The face of my Beloved filled my mind. Her last words to me... A million..."A million," I typed. "A MILLION."

They sucked in a collective breath.

"You drive a hard bargain, but... a month? Oh, a million a year! Yes. Sure. Which reminds me guys," said Barney looking around the Golden Circle at his Independent Directors, "While we're all here, might as well appoint Westcom's ruthlessly independent Remuneration Committee."

Fred, Ted and Ned nodded, and pointed around the ring at several men in similar suits.

"Brad?" said Fred.

"Vlad?" said Ted.

"Dad?" said Ned.

Those named nodded and murmured, "Honoured to serve," "For the Greater Good," "With ruthless independence, son."

Barney smiled. "Good choices. Ruthlessly independent men. Stellar CEOs. True Stars."

They blushed. "Thanks Barney!" sang the new Independent Remuneration Committee in sweet harmony.

"Fourball Thursday?" said Barney.

"Sure thing, Barney!" they sang. Bill Gates and a Capitalist with Chinese Characteristics suddenly joined in, with nimble operatic notes.

"Ah, the Opera!" said Barney. "Bill and I, and Chen Chonghuang... Chen dominates the global Mask industry..." Chen

Chonghuang nodded to me from the far end of the table. "…we sing each year, in a charity opera, in Seattle…" Barney and Bill and Chen Chonghuang sang a rapidly ascending scale in bass, tenor, and baritone respectively. "But now we give thanks for the coming of a new millennium…"

"A Thousand Years," their murmur drifted around the table, "A Thousand Years…"

"…in which to exercise our humble talents, for modest reward, in the service…"

"Service!"

"Service!"

"…of Corporate Capitalism. Oh, just a little Thanksgiving Snack."

I frowned. "Millennium?" I typed. It was not for another couple of years yet. "MILLENNIUM?" came my robot voice.

Barney smiled. "We are busy servants of Capital. This was the only day we all had free from the crushing burden of running our Publicly Listed Companies for the Good of the Shareholders. In fact…" Now Barney frowned across the table. "Might be a good time for a pay review, guys?"

"Sure thing, Barney!"

Barney frowned further. "Be ruthlessly Independent, now, guys. Rigorous."

"Sure thing, Barney!"

Barney unfrowned. "Great. Fourball on Friday?"

"Sure thing, Barney!"

"Great." Barney hauled a great wad of banknotes from his pocket. "Here's my last pay packet. Review it." He tossed it to Brad.

Brad lofted it in his hand a few times and frowned. "Light, very light…"

Brad tossed it to Vlad, who frowned, and shook his head, and tossed the packet to Ned's Dad.

"And when you've done mine," said Barney, "Make sure you

get your own Independent Remuneration Committee to do yours, to bring you into line."

I looked away. I needed to concentrate. Prepare. What else? The lads had been asked Questions. What questions? They had been asked could they read and write. Yes, yes, excellent. I knew the answer. And where did they see themselves in five years time... more difficult, that. I frowned.

Barney smiled. "Meanwhile, gentlemen, if you have any questions to ask the candidate for the post of consultant on Westcom's newest, ah, project..."

There was a brief silence.

Barney's pay packet continued to pass from hand to hand, faster and faster round the circle. As it moved faster and faster, relative to me, it seemed, by some process I could not fully understand, to grow more and more massive.

"So," said one of the Star CEOs, who was also one of Barney's fourball partners. "What is your Handicap?"

My Handicap? I drooled and twitched, sideways, in my chair, unsure how best to answer. But the others hissed, and shushed and booed him, and I did not have to answer the question. Blushing, and stuttering apologies, he stood, and stumbled backwards away from the table.

The Star, accelerating away from me, grew redder and redder, before disappearing into the black.

There was another silence.

Bill Gates cleared his throat. "So," said Bill Gates, staring at me. "Professor Hawking..." I smiled sideways, and hoped the question would not be too hard. An easy question, please make it an easy question... Bill Gates smiled back. "Could you explain to us the Theory of Relativity?"

The others cheered and whistled their approval.

"Yeah!" "Go, Einstein!" "Always wanted to know." One suited man frowned. "Nothing too complicated. Use terms a five-year-old child can understand." "Yeah!" "Yeah!" "Yeah!"

"Bring me a five-year-old child!" cried Barney O'Reilly Fitzpatrick McGee. There was a stirring in the darkness beyond the light. "It is important to Benchmark your Performance," explained Barney. "After all, the Shareholders' Money, our Sacred Trust, is at stake."

They all leaned forward, staring at me. I attempted to clear my throat. This was a thing I had not been prepared for by the physics textbooks of the Brothers of Jesus Christ Almighty, which cut off abruptly at Copernicus. Here we go, I thought. A million lay in the balance. And with it True Love, my future happiness… I tried to put it out of my mind.

"One million at stake here," said Barney. "So just relax…. A million… and a place in the Golden Circle… hanging on this answer… no pressure….A millllllllllion…"

I twitched and nodded under the powerful influence of the glue, which was burning in my nostrils. I felt the desire to sneeze a mighty sneeze but, gripping the arm of the chair, fought it back.

Must… concentrate…

I was distracted as a small, female, five-year-old child, wide-eyed with wonder, was led up onto the stage by a tall, silent woman with long dark hair worn loose.

I sat, transfixed by the face of the silent woman and by my various impediments.

"Who…" I typed, looking sideways at the woman, "is She?" "WHO… IS… SHE?"

"Who?" said Barney, trying to follow my eyeline, and arriving in error at the child. "Oh, her. A genetic defect holds her eyes permanently Wide Open in Wonder at the World. We have to keep spraying her corneas lest they dry and crack."

The child looked up at him, Wide-Eyed with Wonder.

"I am Erica," she said.

He sprayed her in the eyes.

"She's probably the cutest kid in the world. A little Asian…"

"But not *too* Asian," said Chen Chonghuang.

"A little White…"

"But not *white bread*," said Bill Gates.

"…You've probably seen her on TV," said Barney. "Mostly she's the kid in the background of political and cultural Photo Opportunities, signifying Relevance, Youth, Modernity and Ethnicity. She," he tousled her hair, "Adds Value."

The child looked up at him, Wide-Eyed with Wonder.

The silent woman with the extraordinary face moved silently back into the shadows, looking back at the child and the men. Her face…

"So," said Barney, "Explain Relativity to the kid so she can understand it, and the Million is yours."

"Hey, Professor Hawking," said the five year old child, wide-eyed with wonder.

Barney leaned across the table and sprayed her corneas.

"You were cool in the Simpsons," said the child. "I did Relativity with my Mom, so I know some of this stuff already, but there's a couple of things I don't understand…"

Beads of sweat broke out upon my brow. What was Relativity? Something to do with Relatives. What Relatives? Her mom? Oh, to have a Mom! The glue blurred my vision, and clouded my thoughts. "So," said the five-year-old girl, from the far side of the circle. "What is a photon?"

Concentrate… I was distracted by Barney's massive Packet as it passed from hand to hand around the table in front of me. The packet had now reached such a speed that it blurred, and formed a translucent line rising and falling from hand to hand. I tried to follow the individual packet with my eye, but could not tell if I was observing a Wave or a Particle. Having gotten into the habit of typing my thoughts, I absently typed, "It has the characteristics of both a Wave and a Particle, depending on how you choose to observe it…" My robotic voice abruptly spoke. "IT HAS THE CHARACTERISTICS OF BOTH A WAVE AND A PARTICLE, DEPENDING ON HOW YOU CHOOSE TO

OBSERVE IT."

To my bewilderment, the Independent Directors applauded. "Good answer." "Even I understood that."

She nodded, and said, "I would like to know everything about the electron."

"Hah! Tricky," said the Directors, and passed Barney's pay packet ever faster, round the Golden Circle. Sweat broke out on their brows.

Bill Gates frowned, and murmured, "These questions are largely quantum physics, and not, strictly speaking, Relativity... out of his field, and a little unfair... but let it stand, he is doing well."

"Everything?" I typed, to gain a little time. "EVERYTHING?" If I could only concentrate... this infernal glue...what on earth was an electron? Think!

But my attention was still held by the packet. By flicking my eyes in the direction of its direction, I could glimpse it, solid, for an instant, but lost the sense of its movement... "It is possible to know its position: or its state: but not both at the same time," I typed. "IT IS POSSIBLE TO KNOW ITS POSITION; OR ITS STATE; BUT NOT BOTH AT THE SAME TIME."

The Independent Directors cheered.

Wide-Eyed with Wonder, Erica said, "Well, how fast can a particle go? Is there a top speed? And if so, why?"

All leaned forward. But I was still held transfixed by the behaviour of Barney's pay packet, which did not seem to be obeying the normal rules of the everyday world. Yet it did follow a fundamental logic all its own. And so I typed, "As it goes faster and faster, relative to me, it appears to grow more and more massive... So that it becomes harder and harder to accelerate it... for it takes more and more energy to increase the speed of its increasing mass..." For the Independent Remuneration Committee were sweating now as they heaved the massive packet round the golden ring.

They gasped as my words emerged, and turned to stare at the girl, murmuring "But has she really understood it?"

The five-year-old girl fell into silent thought. But my attention now drifted to Barney. It seemed to me that Barney somehow, was the Ring Master of this Golden Circle. I could not see how he was doing it, for he did not touch his pay packet, which was being reviewed with Ruthless Independence by a totally Independent Remuneration Committee... Yet somehow, I could not shake off the notion that on some higher level, he influenced the process, orchestrated it, conducted it, exerted an invisible force that did not drop off over distance... I felt on the brink of a fundamental breakthrough... That Barney was not just the Master of this particular Ceremony, but Master of Ceremonies at some higher level; to some higher power... my exhausted fingers could not type all that... The girl, having done her thinking, looked up. All stared at her.

She spoke. "You seem to be saying that Energy... is somehow equivalent in some way to Mass... which... wow! Would imply that there is a Constant speed faster than which nothing, not even a photon of light, can go!"

"My God," said the Independent Directors, "He has led her cunningly to discover for herself the fundamental law of the Universe..."

I suddenly understood everything. "He," I thought, and tried to type in urgent shorthand, my finger missing a letter in my haste, "is equal to the Master of Ceremonies, squared."

Her light, low voice made harmony with my harsh robotic boom as we both cried aloud together, "$E=MC^2$!"

As all around me cheered, I watched as Barney quietly pulled open the immense dark maw of his trouser pocket. The pay packet of Barney O'Reilly FitzPatrick McGee, having been Independently Reviewed, was now so astonishingly massive that it could be accelerated no further, relative to me. Unobserved by anyone else, the massive object entered the Black Hole, and vanished.

At the far side of the Golden Circle, the extraordinarily beautiful woman reappeared. I had earned a Million; I had fulfilled half my Quest; I was on the brink of winning my True Love; yet this silent woman sent a shiver through me that left me thoughtful and unsure.

The silent woman took the five-year-old child by the hand, and led the child and my heart away, into darkness.

At that moment the Snack arrived.

"Would you like to Join us?" said Bill Gates, turning to me.

"It's nothing formal..." said Chen Chonghuang.

"Just throw all those lobsters into that trough...." said Barney O'Reilly Fitzpatrick McGee.

21.

After the Thanksgiving Snack, the Titans talked.

Barney wiped his lips. "In less than two years America will elect a new King, for the new Millennium, and his father's courtiers have told me that when he is King he will want a new System, to Defend the Realm. And also to expand it slightly." He loosened his belt one notch, and continued. "We at Westcom are to design our System, and prepare our bid, but we need a piece of Software to handle the extraordinary quantities of information pouring in from satellite and spy, radar and report, weather and politics, in order to distill an order to fire. And, indeed, to choose what to fire at. Do any of you recall the Corporation you humbly serve owning a subsidiary with such a product?"

All frowned, and winced, and scratched head and buttock.

A dim nerve twitched in my brain.

"In short," said Barney O'Reilly Fitzpatrick McGee, "we seek synthetic Wisdom."

Brilliantly, I saw how to make amends to Pat Sheeran for my earlier indiscretions. "The One you Seek," I typed, "Is Pat Sheeran. His Salmon of Knowledge will do all you desire."

Silence filled the Hall.

Barney O'Reilly Fitzpatrick McGee leaped in his seat: "Whoops, I had forgotten you were there," he said. "Pat Sheeran, you say? Why, the very fellow sought a meeting with me today. I had been about to turn him down, for no Person of Political Importance seemed to know him. But if the Einstein of the Age recommends his Product... Well, I shall give it a fair trial."

I could not reveal my true identity to Barney. But I wished to let Pat Sheeran know that I had made amends... Hmmm... tricky but doable. "Do not," I typed, "reveal my name to Pat Sheeran. Merely tell him that the person who recommended his mighty Device is sorry for pissing on the Minister before he got a chance to give her one."

"Egad," said Barney, "You Europeans. I cannot entirely hide my noble and idealistic American disgust at the perverse relationship between business and politics here. But OK." Silent waiters cleared the table. "And now, excuse me gentlemen, but I must show our new Consultant what it is we will be working on."

He wheeled me down a ramp, off the platform. The entire thing, office and all, now rose silently up into the darkness as the Titans waved goodbye, toasting him in fizzy wine.

"To next year!"

"To the next Century!"

"A Thousand Years!" sang Chen Chonghuang.

They vanished above. The spotlights dimmed.

The vast space stood revealed.

22.

The cavern extended around us in a great arc, almost to the limits of vision. From it led corridors or tunnels travelling an unknown distance further into the rock. Closer to us, white-coated figures moved smoothly about well-equipped open workspaces. There was a great deal of delicate machinery, many objects resembling microscopes, and on every desk the glowing screens of Televisions, attached to Typewriters. A female figure approached us rapidly from the far distance. There was something compelling about her walk.

"Impressive, huh?" said Barney. "Westcom is officially divided into eight units: voice recognition, fibre optics, localisation, yadda-yadda-yadda. This," he indicated the vastness about us, "is the Ninth. The Black Unit. Nobody knows these people are here. Including these people. They pretty much all believe they're still back home." He tipped me a wink. "Best not to disillusion them."

The woman was closer now. The silent dark-haired woman. Her beauty grew crisper and more focused as she approached. Her black hair was tied back under a white cap, her eyes, green even at this distance, shone behind tiny glasses with no frames. Her pale skin glowed. I could feel my heart stir painfully. Not just my heart. I grew confused, for had I not already lost my heart to my one True Love? How could these stirrings be?

I felt a great pang of longing for the quiet embrace of the Orphanage, where my heart was my own and there was none to interfere with its calm.

She… she turned aside, to mutter something into the ear of a male colleague at one of the benches, and I observed the exquisite undulations of her profile. My manhood lurched in my lap but, caught down the left leg of my trousers, could not find a position of ease.

I groaned aloud.

"You've noticed they're mostly Black, huh?" said Barney.

I looked closer, and saw that most of the faces around me were indeed unusually tanned for an underground Irish workforce in mid-winter.

Barney nodded. "Might be the last generation of authentic, home-grown Blacks to work for Westcom, and I'll tell you why…" He looked about the great space, and a drop of moisture swelled in the corner of each eye.

I settled back in my chair. I liked a story.

He blew his nose, and cleared his throat. "Back when old man Fitzpatrick grew tobacco, the procuring of labour was an arduous, expensive, time-consuming business. Black men had to be sourced and purchased from unscrupulous Arab middlemen and imported by ship from West Africa. Spoilage rates were as high as 50%. Oh, times were tough for old man Fitzpatrick. Sure, eventually we had sufficient spare capacity to provide a breeding stock, and we were self-sufficient in labour. But then the cost of raising our African workers fell entirely on our family: a Manifestly Unfair Situation. Often we'd get a good crop of sturdy young Blacks raised up to five or six years of age, near enough ready to do productive work and repay our investment: and they would all sicken and die in the sheds, and we had all the weary work to do all over again. The situation was intolerable, it was against natural justice: and so we campaigned for the abolition of slavery."

I nodded my approval of this virtuous campaign.

"Came the glorious day, and we could kick them all out and they could rear their own brats on their own time, and their own dime. We rehired them, as needed, when they had matured. This improved profitability enormously. Productivity shot up too, for now the workers no longer had a cushy berth for life. The excess money saved, we invested in mining and smelting the iron ore in the hills too steep for cultivation. But, for that, a steady supply of strong male labour was required. We couldn't be willy-nilly hiring by ones and twos. And so we contracted with the local prisons to supply our needs. They sourced the male labour as required. A vagrancy sweep, or a crackdown on gambling would supply peak labour demand at the mine. By now we were Western American Steel... But pretty soon we were paying so much out to the prisons for convict labour that we had a change of heart. Old grandpappy Fitzpatrick built our first prison. And so you see we could get the State, then later as we expanded into Federal Prisons, the Federal Government to pay to feed and house our workers, and we could pay ourselves for their services. So *we* were getting paid for *them* to work for *us*. It was soon our most profitable unit... You may have heard of our correctional subsidiary, American Stars 'n' Bars? Our Patriot Prison? With its uniquely flexible modular system?"

"Hmm?" I had been watching the green-eyed woman, who was very carefully taking something out of a safe and transferring it to a silver container that bounced light across her cheekbones, her noble nose... I shook my head, though as my head was on its side this involved rotating my face vertically rather than horizontally relative to the surface of the earth. Barney tilted his head in sympathy with mine.

"That's a...Yes. Ha ha. Are you nodding or...? Ha ha... Anyway, as WAS became Westcom, and our jobs moved up the value chain, our prisoners, chiefly Negroes of little educational attainment, simply weren't cutting it. Oh, they were bright and willing, but training them up costs time and money, and these guys simply weren't inside long enough to make the investment worthwhile. They were missing out on training opportunities, the chance of betterment... Why, it was a crime. No, it was worse than a crime: it was a tragedy. So we lobbied Congress long and hard to give us *time* to really make a difference to these young men's lives. And so we got their sentences doubled."

I nodded, sideways, and stared at the face of the dark haired, green eyed woman. Head bowed over the silver container, staring into its depths.

"...But as Westcom became a favoured contractor on Federal Government Defence contracts, and we came to understand the Federal Government better, we came to... if I may use the word... *love* the Federal Government. And we began to feel concern for its welfare. One has to see the bigger picture, and take the longer view. As the Federal Government pays us up to $500 for a screwdriver on our Defence contracts, it makes sense to maximise the State's revenues so that they can pay us... Thus, if we can lower the burden on the Government, we can increase our income and profitability. And our prisoners are fine, fine, people. But they cost the Government a fortune in benefits, in healthcare and education, in providing street-lighting to their ghettos and so forth, before they are old enough to graduate to prison. It is the old problem my ancestor faced, of covering the overhead on their unproductive years. So the *future* lies in outsourcing labour to foreign slave-states. Let the Chinese and Hindus and so forth raise the whining infants to maturity. *Not on America's tab...* We will build our prisons abroad, and ship the goods home. Indeed, we have used this opportunity to rethink the entire prison paradigm. In our next-generation foreign prisons, the prisoners will be kicked out after their shift and will have to feed and house themselves at their own expense. It is quite, quite brilliant, and will enhance profitability threefold... And so these are the last, I fear, of the great Black American workforce which my family has served so proudly and so humbly for so long. Here, meet some, before they vanish, like the Buffalo..."

He waved, and two young men in dark suits walked over to us. Barney whispered in my upturned ear, "Lately many of them have discovered Religion. I have encouraged it, for it makes them more Punctual, but Christ Almighty, they tend to go on about it... Gentlemen! I'd like you to meet Professor Stephen Hawking."

"Sir."

"Sir."

I asked them about their religion. Barney groaned.

"Well sir, we are brothers in the Brotherhood of Brothers of Muhammad in the Hood."

"Followers of the teachings of Muhammad…"

"It is a little known fact that Muhammad was a Black man, of Africa…"

"It is a little known fact that the first man to whom the Prophet gave the honour of giving the Call to Prayer was a freed Black slave, Bilal…"

"And so we follow that great Religion…"

"A Religion blind to the colour of a man's skin."

"A Religion of compassion."

"Religion of Love."

"Religion of tolerance."

"For the Prophet taught us to hate no-one."

"And thus we hate no one."

"Except the fucking Mexicans."

"Yeah the Mexicans. And the fucking Koreans."

"Fucking Koreans. And whitey."

"Yeah, whitey."

"Fuck the Man."

"And the cops."

"Fuck the cops."

"Nothing worse than a black man in a cop jacket."

"*Fuck* those negroes."

"Yes, fuck them."

"Thank you, gentlemen," said Barney.

"Sir."

"Sir."

They bowed and left.

"Oh well, it's better than Marxism," said Barney.

The woman with green eyes finally arrived, bearing aloft a silver salver covered with a silver dome.

"The Goo, Father." She swept a strand of loose hair back from her face, behind her delicate ear.

I started in my chair.

"Why, I never introduced you," said Barney. "My daughter Babette, Professor Stephen Hawking."

"Professor Hawking." She bowed fractionally, casting her green eyes down to my lap. "You are somewhat... larger, than you appear on television."

I blushed so strongly that I felt a little dizzy.

"Show Steve the Goo, Babette," said Barney. "And explain."

"I am a materials scientist, in charge of the microchip materials research group's workshop," said Babette.

I nodded, having recognised the words "chip" and "shop". What was the peculiar charm of chip shop girls, I wondered? Was it the job made them charming or their charm that drew them to the job? I gazed at her. Her haunting eyes confused themselves with my memory of those of my true love, and my lad leapt in my lap.

With one graceful movement, she removed the silver lid from the silver salver and placed its cool dome over my restless crotch. Her tact entranced me. My blushes faded.

"This," said the President of Westcom, "Is the Goo."

Babette lowered the silver salver till I was looking down upon it. On it stood a silver bowl, brimful of a liquid precisely the colour of her eyes. I stared into its green depths.

"We discovered it," said Babette, "by mistake, after a series of errors, while developing a non-silicate substrate..."

"This, Stephen," said Barney, "will change the world. It is a room temperature super-conductor which will hold any amount of electric charge indefinitely. It offers no resistance..." He continued to talk as I looked up from the bowl of Goo into the heavens of Babette's eyes.

"We have managed to manufacture a single Ring from the Goo," she said, and produced it. She raised it to my eye, that I might see it close.

I looked at her through its softly glowing iris. She looked at me.

I blinked.

"We are trying to back-engineer the process which created it, but it seems complex…"

"Beautiful, isn't it?" said Barney. Yes, I typed with fingers which trembled with the Palsy of Awe.

"YELKSH…" said my Computer Voice.

Babette smiled at me. "I believe my father is referring to the Goo," she said in a voice like silken stockings sliding down a golden thigh. "It is still highly unstable in the presence of solvents. It undergoes a catastrophic explosive decomposition. This whole research hall has to be kept clear of epoxies, benzene-ring evaporative cleansers… We can't even glue the chairs back together. Everything must be welded or screwed."

"Crazy paranoia from the Health & Safety guys 'n' gals, of course," said Barney. "It'd take a whole tube of glue, as well as a heat source, to set off this baby."

Babette smiled down at me. "Here," she said, "Feel it," and she took my hand and slipped my forefinger into the tight, warm ring.

The dome stirred in my lap.

"I see you are interested," she said.

I nodded vigorously, dislodging the enormous clod of glue blocking my right nostril. At the tickle of its shifting, I gasped a huge long-delayed breath, and sneezed with extraordinary violence. The clod of hard glue in my left nostril held firm, while an astonishing quantity of still-liquid glue was projected down the barrel of my right nostril, to spatter and splash the glowing meniscus of Goo.

"Sweet Jesus, Hawking," said Barney, his cigar dropping from nerveless fingers. "Is that an epoxy glue I smell?"

I was not entirely sure what kind of poxy glue it was. Distracted by the anguish and ecstasy of my heart, I said nothing. Babette frowned, and took a step behind the vast bulk of Barney.

The cigar landed on its burning tip in the centre of the boiling, glue-covered surface of the now fuming Goo.

The resulting explosion blew me back up the lift shaft. As I passed the Desk again, my head on fire, accelerating ever upward, the problems of my Heart became entirely Academic...

23.

I awoke in Hospital, bandaged like a Mummy of Ancient Egypt. Pale fluids gurgled down a tube and disappeared into my bandaged arm, while dark fluids gurgled out of a second tube from my bandaged Nether Regions. I studied this second tube with concern, and not a little distress. Looking away, I saw a copy of the Galway Advertiser, lying on the bedside locker. The date printed on it was several weeks into the future.

But how...? Could it be that...?

It took me some time to realise I had been carried by the great river of time, while unconscious, several weeks into the future, rather than the Newspaper having been carried by a more mysterious route several weeks into the past. A great pity, for it contained the Lotto numbers. My sigh of disappointment, through a throat dry and crackly with neglect, drew the attention of the bandaged figure in the bed beside mine.

"Miguel de Navarra," said the bandaged man. "I would shake your hand, were I not in traction. You are the mysterious revolutionary stranger who blew up Westcom's Black Section, no?"

"Sorry," I said.

"Do not fear, I have told no one," said Miguel de Navarra. "To disguise yourself as Professor Stephen Hawking was quite brilliant, and to blow up your own self in your attempt to strike at the Yankee oppressor was heroic. I would salute you, were I not in traction. I, too, was blown up the lift shaft alongside you. But I have said nothing. Nothing! Their interrogators have got nothing from my lips."

"They have interrogated you?"

"No. But it is only a matter of time. I would offer you a Kiwi Fruit," he said, nodding at a bowl on his bedside locker, "but unfortunately they have been watered with the blood of the workers."

Perhaps ten minutes later, as my neighbour began to get into his stride on the subject of the working conditions of the fruit ranches of the imperial Yankee oppressor in Central America, I found my attention wandering back to the Galway Advertiser.

GALWAY PENSIONER'S WATERSUPPLY TO COST
£8,524,000

I read.

Scenes of disorder in the County Council chambers greeted the news last Monday of a cost overrun on the supply of drinking water to a pensioner in the Connemara region. 'We contracted to supply the aforementioned pensioner with running water,' said Councillor Flahavan (Fianna Fáil). 'It was then ascertained that the said pensioner lived twenty eight miles offshore, on a rock. This led to cost overruns of approximately 14,000%.' Councillor Flahavan's statement was greeted by uproar in the chamber. Certain allegations were made by Councillor Michael D. Higgins (Labour), to cries of 'Shame!' from the Fianna Fáil members. A developer's name was mentioned. The restoration of order was accompanied by the eviction from the chamber of Councillor Higgins.

I was not entirely sure why this story was holding my attention so firmly. My neck felt stiff. My head felt peculiar. Indeed, all of me felt peculiar. A peculiar drowsy numbness mingled with a peculiar sharp focus. And things had the most peculiar edges, and my head felt made of peculiar cloth.

Miguel de Navarra attempted to draw my attention to the lack of curvature of Guatemalan bananas with a vivid metaphor: "Stretched upon the rack of the Imperial Oppressor." I nodded vaguely, and read on with calm, disinterested fascination.

> Upon the restoration of order, Councillor Flahavan continued by saying, 'However, by closing Barna National School, cancelling plans to make Galway wheelchair-friendly, and capping the expense account of the Arts' Officer, we have made good the shortfall and the budget will show a modest surplus for the year.' General applause greeted this announcement and the budget was passed by nine votes to nil, with one abstention.

Reading on, I discovered a smaller item in tiny print in the bottom right hand corner of the page.

WESTCOM EXPLOSION REPORT: INVESTIGATORS BAFFLED

read the headline.

WILL NOT AFFECT TOURIST NUMBERS, SAYS COUNCILLOR

I leaned further out of bed into the light to read on, resulting in a fearsome tug to my Organ, which I now discovered to be firmly attached to the second tube. A groan of some anguish escaped me.

"He's awake!" came a voice from the doorway, and within seconds every Doctor in the Hospital surrounded me. A Tall Doctor, a Short Doctor, a Brown Doctor, a Lady Doctor...

The cries of suddenly-abandoned patients in traction echoed down the lonely corridors.

Only the Lady Doctor held my attention, for her astonishing beauty reminded me of my Beloved. Anguish filled me. The explosion! With trembling fingers, I felt my bandaged face.

"Am I... disfigured? For life?" I asked.

The Tall Doctor spoke cautiously. "You were very badly injured in the explosion, sir. Your general skin-surfaces we saved by the use of a revolutionary hi-tech material, developed here in Ireland by the Westcom corporation..." All applauded. "But your nose... The loss of skin and cartilage... Well, we had to entirely rebuild your nose with undamaged skin and tissue grafted from the only part of your body protected from the blast..."

"A pioneering operation!" interrupted the Short Doctor.

"Unprecedented!" burst in the Brown Doctor.

Only the Lady Doctor said nothing, her great grey eyes, like pools of moonlit water, drawing me in to bathe in their wordless comfort. I floated upward to her on a wave of love and painkillers, and fell out of my Bed.

The beautiful Doctor caught me as I fell. I found myself gazing down the loose front of her Blouse, and discovered that her pert Breasts required no Brassiere to keep them firm and buoyant. Pleasant sensations ran the length of my nose. Her cool hands cupped my Bandaged Buttocks as she gently lifted me back into bed. To my astonishment, my rebuilt nose began to rise to a quite unprecedented angle, and to grow in length and width. Stitches snapped, crackled, and popped. My nose, enormous now, filling

76

my vision, rose yet further to brush against her long hair and, filling swiftly with the most exquisitely pleasurable sensations, began to Throb like a... like a great... like an enormous...

"Oh dear," said the Doctors. "We hadn't thought of that."

24.

Thus began a strange period in my life.

Much of what they fed down the pale tube into my arm was Morphine, and so a featureless yet pleasant expanse of time drifted by me without my paying it much attention. The rhythm of the weeks was laid down only by the arrival each Thursday of the Galway Advertiser, which boasted the Largest Audited Circulation of any free newspaper in Ireland. The delivery children would swiftly haul their laden trolleys the length of the ward, thrusting a paper into the broken arms or under the bandaged buttocks of each shattered patient. Then they'd be off, singing, down the corridor to the neo-natal intensive care unit, to thrust papers into the incubators. And I would know another seven days had passed.

My neighbour Miguel would turn straight to the Situations Vacant column and study it intently, gasping and groaning. I quizzed him once on this.

"You seem un-attracted to the jobs on offer."

"On the contrary: it is my ambition to get a Shit Job. Ideally, as a security man in a Gated Community of the Rich, that on a daily basis I may see those better off than me, flaunting their wealth and, hopefully, treating me with indifference - or, even better, contempt."

"This seems to me a low ambition for a Revolutionary who has been jailed Thrice for his radical student activities."

"Ah, but it will fuel my revolutionary zeal," he said, "For it has been flagging of late. I need to have my nose rubbed in the inequalities of Capitalism."

"But surely working as Convict Labour for Westcom fuelled your revolutionary zeal?"

"Well..." He looked at his toes, and twiddled them. "No... The work was interesting and the management structure flat and non-hierarchical. It became difficult to find a focus for my Revolutionary Rage."

"That is a pity," I said.

"Yes," he said, and went back to the Advertiser Classifieds.

With much effort, over many weeks, I learned to control my rebellious Nose. In this task, the Lady Doctor took a special interest. She frequently lent a cool and helpful hand, though the caress of that hand was often enough to send my nose rocketing aloft.

"There, there," she would murmur, as I tried to control my excitable wild nose by doing complicated sums in my head. The excitement would finally pass, and my nose would return to its placid state.

I grew to love the Lady Doctor, for her beauty and her kindness. Indeed, sometimes her hand moved thoughtfully up and down my nose as though she, too, felt emotions too great for words. Yet within me burned a terrible guilt. For had I not promised my heart to another? Was I so fickle a fellow as to forget my True Love, and the task she had set me to win her hand?

And to my shame I found, in my unguarded moments, visions of Babette overwhelming me in the most curious and disturbing fashion. Indeed, on occasion, the Underground chip-shop girl and the Overground chip-shop girl blended limbs and tongues and lips in languid combinations in my warm and drugged imagination for what seemed like hours.

Torn between beauties, I cursed Galway, City of Sin! Such dilemmas were entirely unknown in Tipperary, home of my happy Orphanage days, for there we were all as Ugly As Dogs Walking Backwards.

I set myself against such confusing reveries, and I vowed to nurture the pure flame of my First Love, and be no more distracted from my quest. She was out there somewhere, waiting for me. Pining. She... believed in me.

No, completing the sacred task she had set me would occupy my every waking moment till she was mine.

25.

The completion of one half of my sacred task proved easier than I could have imagined. The rebuilding of my face was still in its earliest stages, and there was much doubt and debate among the doctors as to how to proceed. I was asked to describe my face by means of drawings, clay models, and Pictures on a Television, as they had no photograph of me to guide their reconstruction. By judicious choice of the correct cheekbones, lips and chin, I was able surreptitiously to have my face rebuilt in the very image of Leonardo DiCaprio, on the National Health Service of Ireland. The Lady Doctor eyed my bandaged face thoughtfully as I described my Movie Star looks, but she did not argue with my choices, although the Short Doctor tried to talk me out of the dimple.

Slowly the weeks became months.

Miguel gradually mended. Eventually he was able to sit up unaided, and, attempting to hurl an ideologically unsound orange across the Ward at a foe, fell out of bed and broke the other leg and arm.

My original penis and scrotum, from which had been taken thin strips of tissue for my facial grafts, soon healed. My new face began to emerge from the surgery and bandages. Everywhere else, my new Westcom skin had re-grown on my old body and Doctors would come to stroke it and marvel. The skin was smooth and delightful and very young and I no longer needed to shave. My long neck, too, was marvellously flexible again, after skilful reconstruction, and I could turn my head a full 180 degrees. I could walk my drip-stand to the toilet now, and would stand there, blinking at the familiar stranger in the mirror until it slowly sank in that it was me.

I was the Living Spit of Leonardo DiCaprio, though with an erectile nose.

But, as further weeks went by and the nasal capillaries grew and the deeper blood vessels repaired, my nose filled out and my cheekbones vanished. Soon only the application of cold water from the sink could tighten and shrink the gristle of my nose and the smooth scrotal skin of my rebuilt cheeks into the button nose and prominent cheekbones of Mr. DiCaprio...

And then, one day, I saw my Beloved again.

I was taped, at the time, to a Monitor, my emotions being Judged by a stern Machine.

"That," said the Lady Doctor pointing, "is your Heart."

A bright green line moved in a smooth wave across the screen. I smelt a warm Perfume as she moved, so like that of my distant Beloved... The green line thundered, but I quickly solved a quadratic equation, and it stilled. And yet... The Short Doctor had left the room to answer the visitors' bell. We were alone at last...

"That is a beautiful Perfume," I said to the Lady Doctor.

"I do not wear perfume," she replied.

There came a banging upon the door, strangely regular. A mightier Bang thrust it open, to reveal Her, My Beloved, to whom I had promised my heart.

She appeared to be attempting to resuscitate a naked, groaning man, by sitting astride him and bouncing up and down on his chest. Perhaps not his chest. Somewhat lower. It was the Short Doctor, who appeared now to be suffering a Fit beneath her.

My excitement was great. My nose rose in delight. Here was the source of that warm Perfume. My Beloved! Here! Saving lives.

I stared at the Lady Doctor with wild surmise.

"Oh," said the Lady Doctor, "It's that new Tart from the Canteen."

"That," I said stiffly, "is the woman I intend to make Mine."

"Well, you're in with a good chance," said the Lady Doctor. "She is an Absolute Slapper and would Get Up On Anything."

The Short Doctor gave a great cry, and my Beloved a greater cry, in rhythm with him.

Understanding dawned on me. And in that moment I watched my heart break into a thousand tiny pieces all across the flickering screen.

26.

I determined to leave the hospital immediately, and have no more to do with women. My clothes having been destroyed, the hospital authorities issued me a pinstripe suit, from the stock of charitable clothing out of which they habitually re-clothed injured street drinkers before their discharge. The lady Doctor attempted to persuade me to stay for a week's further treatment, to stabilise my erectile nose, but I could not bear to stay another hour. When she realised there was no changing my mind, she left me, to return some minutes later with a brown paper bag.

Silently she gave me the eloquent gift of sandwiches, and left the ward without turning back.

I paused only to say good-bye to Miguel de Navarra, my Mexican neighbour. He looked up from the Galway Advertiser and shook my right hand sorrowfully with his right hand.

"This Banana," he said, waving the Illustrative Fruit with his left, "Is a weapon of Oppression."

I nodded. "Can I have it, so?" I said.

I left the hospital with only a brown paper bag full of sandwiches, a banana, and a broken heart.

During the long morphine dream of my stay in hospital, Galway had changed. Most of its buildings had been knocked and replaced with buildings one storey taller. Many of these new buildings were now, in their turn, being replaced with buildings two storeys taller again. I grew confused and lost among the taller storeys and the construction's confusions. All about me as I walked I heard talk of Shares and Options, of New Technologies, Investment Properties, and Easy Money. Galway seemed to be accelerating toward a new millennium in an explosion of optimism and cement dust. Fellow teenagers passed me in Mercedes–Benz cars, often several times, trying in vain to find a place to park.

A shoe-shine boy offered me a share tip as I passed Griffins' Bakery, and the street entertainer, Johnny Massacre, was now swallowing swords of gold.

I finally found Saint Nicholas's Church, my beloved home. I was surprised to see the entire Church of Ireland population of Galway outside it, weeping and wailing in the shelter of a golf umbrella. Far above them, a fat man atop a high ladder was nailing a "SOLD" sign to the Bell Tower. The fat man turned to address the crowd. His lower face was covered by a scarf.

"Feck off," he told them. "It's mine now."

"Who is that masked man?" I enquired.

"'Tis Jimmy O' Bliss," sobbed the pensioner holding the umbrella.

I reeled. Jimmy "Bungle" O'Bliss was Ireland's greatest living Property Developer. No deal of his had ever fallen through. His fame had spread even to Tipperary, where he had bought the abattoir and converted it into luxury eco-friendly apartments, using only paint and plywood. This was the crack ·of doom for Saint Nick's.

O'Bliss descended, the better to address the pensioners.

"Ye selfish bastards! Don't ye care about Galway's homeless?"

He wiped a tear from his eye with a silken 'kerchief. "All those young, unmarried management consultants, without a roof over their heads? Dear God, you people have hearts of stone."

"But 'tis our Church," quavered a pensioner.

"Pah! I bought it fair and square, at auction, for a grand."

"Auction?"

"Look, it's not my fault if somebody forgot to put a reserve on the property. Next thing you'll be telling me it's my fault that the other bidder came down with the flu and broke both his arms."

"The flu doesn't break your arms."

"This flu does."

"But where will we worship? Wed? Baptise?"

"Amn't I providing you with a Portakabin out near Menlo, for the love of God? What more can I do? Do ye want to ruin me, with your religious shenanigans? Have ye any idea what it'll cost me to replace this knackered wreck with decent townhouses, with ground-level Retail Premises? If I hadn't got an offshore client for all these old stones, I'd hardly bother."

"But... what of my Bell Tower, my Home?" I burst out.

"Oh the Bell Tower stays."

I breathed a sigh of relief.

He nodded. "We're enhancing it into a twelve-storey, Swedish, state-of-the-art, automated vehicle-storage tower facility."

"So I can continue living there, then?" I said, in happy confusion.

Jimmy O'Bliss winked at me.

I relaxed.

"No," he said. "It's a fecking carpark, you big gom."

Having lost my Job, my Good Looks and my True Love in swift succession, I had come Home to find that I had also lost my Home. My sandwiches slipped from my fingers to land in the mud, my legs trembled and gave way, and I fell to my knees in the muck and rain...

27.

The National Anthem rang out in thin, high, single notes from the inside pocket of the lumpy navy jacket of Jimmy "Bungle" O'Bliss.

As I knelt, in my devastation, in a puddle, Jimmy O'Bliss high-stepped over me. Pulling a small telephone from his inside pocket, he dislodged a bulging Brown Envelope. It splashed into the puddle in front of me.

A strangely familiar voice came tinny from the tiny telephone, its tone a question.

"I got it, Big Man," replied Jimmy shortly. "Deal's done and dusted." He poked at the little machine, and slid it back into the empty inside pocket.

He stopped. Withdrew his hand. Slapped the pocket.

He stared all around, then down at the ground. With a start and a grunt, he glared at me, then scooped the soaking brown envelope from the muck and thrust it, mud and all, back into his inside pocket.

"You saw nutting," he said, and walked rapidly away.

Wet-kneed, I pulled a disconsolate sandwich from its damp brown wrapper.

My initial bite met with unexpected resistance. I could not recall a tougher crust. I removed it from my mouth to have a look at it. It was green. It had an elastic band around it. I looked at the wet brown paper bag I had taken it out of. It wasn't a bag.

A curious hush had fallen over the crowd. "'Tis the legendary Brown Envelope," whispered one ancient.

I looked back at my sandwich. It wasn't a sandwich.

I gave pursuit.

"Sir!" I cried as I ran.

He did not appear to hear me over the noise of construction. I almost caught up with him on High Street, but the demolition of

Sonny Molloy's shop sent a cloud of dust billowing.

Jimmy O'Bliss vanished.

By the time the rain had damped the dust down, he was gone. There! At the far end of Quay Street.

But when I got there, he had crossed to the Spanish Arch, where a helicopter sat, in the lashing rain, on Buckfast Plaza. Above it was a blur of whirling blades which blew the surface water off the Plaza in a great circle about it, so that it rained sideways, as well as from above, on the young men nearby as they leaped a limestone bench on their rollerskatingboards.

It rained sideways, too, on the woman in black who fed the white Corrib swans that had gathered below her on the river.

The woman in black turned, to stare at me. I took a step towards her. The swans began to swim obliquely away, across the Corrib, towards the Claddagh Basin and its rich sewage outfalls.

Her eyes, now, were all I could see; her body, her face, her head wrapped tightly in black as she stood in the horizontal and vertical rain.

There was something unusual about her eyes...

This woman, I thought, could mean something to me. This woman of whom I know nothing, could tangle her destiny with mine. I merely have to take another step, and speak, and the threads of our destiny cross, and who knows where it will end? Together on some tropical island? In wild flight? In love? In madness?

She stared into my eyes. I shuddered with possibilities. On the blankness of her canvas I painted future after future.

In the distance, the white birds moved, slowly.

She turned, and walked away, over the bridge to the Claddagh, following them obliquely in her vertical rain.

Behind me the helicopter's blades sped up. I turned away from her, to face my horizontal rain.

The helicopter was marked with familiar bold greens. Celtic Helicopters, I thought. The company owned by the family of the much-loved Charles J. Haughey, heroic leader of the Fianna

Fáil Party, former Taoiseach, Celtic Chieftain of all the Gaels, gun-runner, phone-tapper, tax-dodger, fornicator, cute hoor and Saviour of Ireland.

Jimmy O'Bliss leaped aboard, and the helicopter whined and rose immediately.

As I reached it, it was already above my head. Eager both to return the poor man's envelope with its huge wad of banknotes, and to regain my sandwiches, I bounded up onto the limestone bench, scattering the rollerskatingboarders, and leaped high, grabbing with my free hand one of the two fat rails or skis on which it had previously been resting.

I began to regret my rash impulse when the helicopter lurched, turned and began to head out across the water.

The mouth of the river opened into the sea.

The helicopter swung low above the rain-swept wave crests. My weight seemed to tug it lower by the second. My hand began to slip. With my other hand, I crammed the Brown Envelope down alongside the banana in the inside pocket of my pinstripe jacket. Then, with both hands, I hung on.

Dear God, was this the end of me?

Slowly, surely, my strength faded...

As we approached the Aran Islands I made out the black bulk of Inis Mór, then Inis Meáin, then Inis Oírr... Far below me I saw the rusting hulk of an enormous cargo vessel, hurled by storm up the beach and into the rocky fields, long before I was born.

Then we were above the sea again, and into a thick wall of offshore mist. There was no sea and no sky and I had the curious illusion that, were I to let go of the helicopter, I would simply hang where I was, suspended, cushioned on all sides by the cotton wool mist, as the helicopter laboured away from me and vanished.

Cushioned, suspended, no effort, no noise...

My weary fingers began to relax their hold. No! I fought this treacherous vision of comfort, and with numb hands hauled myself higher on the ski, and slung a leg up onto it, and managed, at length, with difficulty, one-handed, to button my jacket around the ski so that my weight was half-supported by my jacket, in which I now hung as in a sling. My aching hands could relax a little.

Then, from out of the mist, loomed the terrible and wonderful shape of the fourth Aran Island.

Hy Brasil...

Yet it did not look right. Its bleak profile should have been familiar from old photographs in the Lifestyle Supplements, back when our Chieftain still gave interviews, before disgrace and self-imposed exile. But no, the familiar dark bulk was half-eclipsed by a great white mountain thrusting out of the water, hard against the island. White fog condensed and rolled off its sides, to form an enormous ring about the white mountain.

The white peak itself, to my exhausted, wind-wracked eyes, seemed to resemble a giant Nose rising from a submerged Face. There were two dark ovals near its peak resembling nostrils. Yes, a Nose sticking up out of the waves. But this, I realised, must be a Neurotic Delusion, caused by the traumatic mutilation of my own nose. I felt delighted at my sophistication. To have acquired my very own Neurosis after so short a time in the Big City! Or, I mused, perhaps I was Hallucinating: an even more sophisti-cated Metropolitan response to reality, and one conferring great status back at the Orphanage. Thady Donnelly had not been right for a week after doing mushrooms on his way to the 1996 All-Ireland hurling semi-finals in Thurles, and the younger orphans had followed him around the Orphanage Grounds, beseeching him to speak of his Visions, till he finally Came Down on the following Friday...

We approached the white peak which masked the dark island. The helicopter flew low over it, and a powerful downdraft sucked us lower still, so that we staggered from the sky to within a few metres of the White Mountain. Even above the Roar of Blades and Engine, I heard Jimmy "Bungle" O'Bliss and the pilot exclaim to their Maker.

The lurching recovery of the helicopter, as it shot back up to a decent height, was good news for the occupants of the helicopter, though of slightly less benefit to me. My numb fingers had been shaken loose by the sudden fall, and all the buttons on my Charity Suit now gave way under the tug of the sudden rise.

For a moment I hung suspended, as the ski-tip caught in my inside jacket pocket... But the pocket ripped.

28.

I fell thrice my height, to strike the White Mountain a glancing blow with my Arse.

The entire mountain rang like a bell, with a hollow, crystal-clear chime. I skidded, bounced, skidded and began to pick up speed as the sloping shoulder of the mountain dropped away beneath me. My sliding descent through the Arctic air grew pleasing to me, and I began to control my course by movements of the shoulders and hips.

Bruised but exhilarated, I hurtled off the last ledge of the iceberg and crashed down to the shingly beach, which was knee-deep in a cushioning layer of slush and fallen ice.

I looked about me, as I brushed the slush from my pinstripe suit. The iceberg almost filled the tiny natural harbour of Hy Brasil.

I turned my back on harbour, iceberg, Aran Islands and Ireland, and walked inland.

The shingly beach became, by imperceptible degrees, stony fields. There were signs of construction work: rough stone channels cut into the unique black limestone of the island and away across the desolate fields.

I looked back, and from this slight elevation could see that the towering mountain of ice was no longer a free-floating berg, but had been pushed or hauled or driven ashore, and up the gently sloping offshore sheet of basalt which surrounded the island.

Why, he is irrigating the fourth Aran Island in the time-honoured way of the nomadic desert peoples of Arabia, I realised. He has towed an iceberg here from the poles. My respect for the genius of Charles J. Haughey grew greater still. Was this not a potent Metaphor for his benign stewardship of Ireland herself? Had he not inherited a desolate island, parched of self-belief, and remade her into an Earthly Paradise flowing with, awash with, drowning in...

I was distracted from my Metaphor by a distant whinnying. Charles J. Haughey's famous string of racing camels! A generous gift to the then-Taoiseach from an Arabian admirer in the 1970s, all Ireland knew their fame. These beautiful beasts reputedly ran wild upon Hy Brasil. Further away again, I heard a curious cracking or crackling noise. It echoed back off the vast North Face of the towering iceberg and mingled with the whinnying, confusing my senses so that I could not make out the direction from which it came. I resolved to head further inland, for it was my vague recollection from the half-remembered Sunday colour supplements that Charles J. Haughey's palatial retirement home was on the far side of the island from the harbour, facing only the bleak Atlantic waves, so that the great man would not have to look upon the Ireland that betrayed him.

I headed directly across the black limestone island, featureless except for the dry stone walls around the dry stone fields and the occasional shallow labourer's grave, cut with a Kango hammer into the raw stone. Here and there, a white arm bone protruded.

The going was extremely difficult, as I scrambled down and up the steep rocky gullies in whose shelter grew ferns and mosses and orchids.

I was breathing heavily when the Salmon unexpectedly leapt in my rear pocket. I hauled it out, and received its Wisdom.

An oblique walk across an area of open crag is a continuous struggle with little cliffs and ridges and gullies, with no two successive steps on the same level, whereas if one follows the direction of the jointing, smooth flagged paths seem to unroll like carpets before one.
-*Tim Robinson, English writer of Irish sympathy, Stones of Aran: Labyrinth, 1995*

Walking with the grain of the landscape, I made far better time.

A thrill of delight ran through my chilled body at the thought that I might soon lay eyes upon the Great Banqueting Hall of our deposed Chief, and that I might be invited to partake in his fabled hospitality.

As I crested the windswept hill I saw, sheltering behind a tall boulder from the wind, the noble profile and imposing brow, the long, sweeping eyelashes and strong jaw, of a racing camel. It turned and gazed with its warm, liquid eyes into my eyes.

"Hullo Camel," I said to it.

It whinnied. There was a crack, another crack, and the noble beast slumped to its knees as though shot.

From the doorway of his palatial retirement mausoleum, former Taoiseach Charles J. Haughey, the smoke curling from the barrel of his rifle, trotted with dainty tread down the broad granite steps and across the gravel. He was followed by the masked figure of Jimmy O'Bliss, and by Dan Bunne, the Supermarket Magnate and one of the great Political Donors of our Age. Our greatest living Retailer, our greatest living Developer and our greatest living Politician! We would have been naked, homeless and ideologically incoherent without them. They had given us so much, no wonder they looked so Wrecked.

"Great shot, Big Man, great shot, head shot, hard shot, great shot," said Dan Bunne, his voice somewhat muffled by his constant chewing on a piece of gum.

"Shut your hole, Bunne, you fucking spastic mong," said Charles J, "You're giving me a fucking headache."

The camel, its eyes now glazed and untenanted, toppled slowly sideways. Charles walked up to the dying beast and, carefully aiming behind its ear, fired a final shot into its brain. The camel's flanks subsided as its last breath shuddered from its throat, rattling its relaxing tongue out of the way in a staccato spray of spittle.

It was not how I had imagined meeting my hero, Charles J. Haughey, but one cannot entirely control one's destiny. I stepped forward and reached for my inside pocket, intending to return the brown envelope full of money to its rightful owner, Jimmy O'Bliss. I cleared my throat.

The three Giants of Old Ireland failed to notice me, Dan Bunne being distracted by a lock of his own matted hair, and the others being distracted by Dan Bunne. The lock of Dan Bunne's hair swung in the breeze, slightly to the right of his right eye. Unable to see it clearly by turning his eyes, he was turning his head.

The hair, being part of his head, turned an equal amount.

He swung around on his heel in an attempt to take the lock of hair by surprise. It remained slightly to the right of his field of vision. He began to pirouette, then reversed direction.

He fell over. Charles J. Haughey sighed.

My fingers, still numb with the cold and locked in a clawlike grip from my helicopter ride, fumbled in my torn jacket pocket for the envelope and grabbed the banana instead, which had become stuck in the lining.

"Shite," I said.

Charles Haughey and Jimmy spun around and saw me for the first time. Dan looked up, blinking and chewing.

Charles Haughey stared at me with the most bloodshot eyes I had ever seen, until I looked down at Dan Bunne's. Their shirts were delightful.

I was pleased that I looked so natty in my pinstriped suit. The bulge of the stuck banana, though, was ruining the cut of my jacket. I tried to jerk it free.

"Drop the gun," said Charles Haughey.

"Gun?" I said, bewildered, and gave another tug on my banana.

"Don't play the innocent with me," said the former Taoiseach. "Freeze."

"I'm already frozen."

"Shut it, funnyman," said Charles J. Haughey.

"He's after the fifty grand," said Jimmy O'Bliss. "I know that fecker from earlier, at Saint Nick's. Oldest trick in the book, kneeling, trying to trip me. He must have followed me in another chopper."

"Which reminds me," said Charles Haughey. "Give me that money for safekeeping while I think what to do with our Mafia chum here."

I began to realise that they had grasped entirely the wrong end of the metaphorical stick.

Jimmy reached into his pocket and brought out a sodden brown paper package. "It fell in a puddle boss, sorry," he said.

Charles J. Haughey grunted and, without taking his eyes off me, ripped open the brown paper with his teeth.

He glanced down at what he held.

"What. The fuck. Is this."

He looked upon my cold toast and chocolate spread sandwiches with a wild surmise. He looked up at me, then across at Jimmy. His eyes grew more bloodshot on the instant, as though a small blood vessel had burst.

"My God. He takes my money and he comes back for more." He looked me up and down with an expression that bore a most curious resemblance to respect.

"I can explain," I said.

"Or die trying."

"I have your money here in my pocket. I merely wish to return it…"

92

"Bollocks. You have a gun in that pocket."

"No, that is a banana."

"Who are you trying to cod? It's a gun."

"A banana."

"Gun."

"Banana."

"Gun."

"Banana."

Dan Bunne had meanwhile stood up, and now chose this moment to spin anti-clockwise upon his left heel, in an attempt to sneak up on his lock of hair from the far side.

He failed. He fell over. His gun went off.

I jerked in reaction, and the banana flew out of my pocket, as Dan Bunne said, "Sweet Jesus Big Man, I've shot myself in the foot!"

Jimmy O'Bliss fell over.

"Oh no, wrong, cancel that, I've shot Jimmy in the foot," said Dan Bunne, and tried to spit out his chewing gum. Nothing emerged but a small quantity of pink spit. "Dear God! I have been chewing my own cheek this past hour!" exclaimed Bunne. "Isn't that gas, now? Hah? Hah? Hah?" He spat more pink spit and had a poke at the inside of his mouth with a jittery finger.

Charles J. ignored him and the yelping Jimmy. "Well, you were telling the truth about that banana. So give me my money."

I delved deeper into my pocket to retrieve the fifty thousand pounds. My fingers slid down, and along the bottom seam, and up the side seam, and out the gaping flap of the ripped, empty pocket.

"You'll never believe what I'm going to tell you," I said to Charles J. Haughey.

Charles took a step towards me, raising his gun, a semi-automatic weapon that appeared custom built. Dan Bunne's long barrelled goose-gun had a magazine big enough to contain a full box of cartridges. Jimmy O'Bliss had just dropped a Browning large-calibre sniper rifle.

"Are such weapons not illegal in the Republic?" I enquired, interested.

"We're not in the Republic now, Pinocchio," said the former Taoiseach, stroking his trigger and stepping closer. "This island is extra-territorial. It's beyond the remit of the glorious fucking Republic."

"Which is handy if you're bringing in workers, and you don't fancy the paperwork…" said Dan Bunne cryptically, with a wink.

"Shut the fuck up, Bunne," said Charles J. Haughey, scowling. He turned back to me. "I am the law here. I am Judge, Jury and fucking Executioner."

A vivid metaphor indeed, I thought. He had not lost his oratorical panache.

"Hang on here a minute," I said.

I picked up my banana, and ran.

29.

Obviously, the pocket had ripped open after being snagged on my fall from the helicopter. The great wad of cash could have slipped out at any point since. My only hope of clearing up this misunderstanding lay in recovering the money from where it had fallen and returning it, as proof of my bona fides. No doubt we would soon be laughing about their ludicrous mistake over a pewter goblet of hot mead. I retraced my route as exactly as possible, hopping into the fern-filled high-walled channels in the limestone and running along them for a while before leaping out and tacking across the grain of the land, leaping the channels at right angles, before dropping back into another for a long, oblique run.

Further and further behind me followed Charles and Dan.

I made it back to the beach with little incident, but there was no sign of the envelope. I clambered from the beach to the iceberg across a shifting mass of collapsed, melting debris.

Cracks and fissures provided hand- and foot-holds in the hard, frictionless surface, and with difficulty, often on all fours, I retraced the path of my easy descent. The ice creaked and cracked beneath me, whole slabs sometimes peeling away as I searched for a solid handhold.

At one point, spread-eagled on the face of a flat cliff of ice, I noticed a curious phenomenon: the ice exploded out in a small spray of shattered fragments just a foot to the left of my head. When I leaned across to look at the strange hole or crater revealed, the same phenomenon took place a foot to the right of my head. I looked back at Charles and Dan to see if they could explain this curiosity, but they seemed busy, a little way up from the base of the iceberg, fiddling with their guns. Not wishing to distract them, I pulled myself up over the lip of the cliff and kept climbing, hidden from them now by the high flank of the berg.

At last, I reached the top:

And there it was, pristine upon the peak: the Brown Envelope, lying where it, and I, had first fallen.

I relaxed and awaited the others' arrival. It had been an exhausting climb, and I was glad of the chance to rest and eat my banana. Though bruised from the morning's events, its flesh was sweet ambrosia to me. I warmed myself with the thought of how relieved and delighted they would be to have their money returned to them.

They seemed a long time coming. Dan Bunne had no doubt been slowed by his unsuitable shoes.

At length I heard their slow, almost cautious approach. "Up here!" I cried. "Come and get it!"

The boom and echo of my voice shook free several ledges of snow, and, disintegrating, they were whirled away down the berg by the chill wind. A split in the ice at my feet widened. I dropped my banana skin into it. The splayed yellow star vanished, tumbling, into the darkness.

A low creak came from the depths.

Charles Haughey's rifle barrel appeared over the ridge, wearing a hat. I laughed at his prank. "Come up here and I'll give it to you!" I shouted, anxious to put the whole embarrassing misunderstanding behind me.

From behind me, I heard the crunch of footsteps on fresh ice crystals. I turned in time to see Dan Bunne appear from over the far side of the frozen peak. He was looking at his feet, stepping carefully around the rim of the enormous nose-holes.

"I'll give it to you right now. You asked for it," I said, reaching for my pocket, "And now you're going to get it."

Dan Bunne swung the long barrel of his goose-gun in my general direction and convulsively pulled the trigger. The massive recoil sent him skidding a full three yards backwards on the smooth leather soles of his Italian shoes. This would not have been so bad had he not been standing two yards from the edge of the Northernmost Hole.

I reached the edge too late to save him. "Dear God!" he cried as he fell. "The Snorter has become the Snorted! It is a judgement on me!"

His hands still gripped the gun, and as he fell he fired, the recoils tumbling him end over end faster and faster till he vanished into the darkness spinning like a Catherine Wheel and emitting great blazing gouts of burning cordite with each report of his weapon until he had exhausted its capacity.

The explosions echoed and re-echoed long after the last blast of flaming gunpowder had scorched the Arctic air. A booming rumble began as the last echoes died, and grew louder. Ice cracked and split far below.

I stepped back from the edge of the Hole as the edge crumbled and fell in. A hairline fracture appeared in the hard ice beneath me. It ran past me in both directions, to the cliff edges.

It widened to an inch, two inches…

The left side of the peak suddenly fell a full foot.

I had a remarkably bad feeling about this.

With awful slowness, the iceberg began to split down the middle.

30.

As the shuddering iceberg began to split, I tried to decide which side of the divide would be the better one to ride out the collapse upon. Yet the great noise made thinking difficult.

My mind was finally made up by the arrival over the ridge of Charles J. Haughey. Perhaps in some way blaming me for the destruction of his iceberg and the death of his oldest friend, he loosed a wild shot at me from close range. I prudently leaped the widening chasm, and found myself falling inland atop a cliff of ice, as Charles J. Haughey's side of the iceberg fell away from me, out to sea.

I wedged myself in a fissure, and endured the accelerating fall.

My half of the split mountain toppled inland, its broad point of contact rolling up the shingly beach and across the stony fields, ever faster, until the very peak slapped against the stony hill crest and snapped off, countless tons of ice now tobogganing down the far slope to overrun the retirement home of Our Great Leader, coming to a halt now in its ruins.

I emerged from my fissure, and slid and fell down off the ice, through the shattered roof, and into the Imperial Bedroom.

I landed upon the plumped, heaped, purple satin pillows.

Sitting at the foot of the bed, bathing his wounded foot, happily untouched by the falling lumber, masonry, and ice, was Jimmy O'Bliss. He looked back at me over his shoulder with an expression I found difficult to interpret, due to the scarf obscuring his lower face.

He stood, and hopped at high speed from the room.

31.

I was delighted by this unexpected chance to return to Jimmy
O'Bliss his packet of money. Still shivering from the icy peak, I
wrapped myself in a beautifully soft sheet of rich Egyptian cotton,
and pursued him down the main stairs, through the banqueting
hall, into the kitchens, down into the cellars, and further down
into the sub-cellars and past a dark tunnel-mouth.

Then back up again.

Finally, as loss of blood slowed the modest and reluctant old
fellow, I cornered him in the banqueting hall. Above us, the
clear glass roof was spangled with chunks of ice, and, above that,
the shuddering overhang of the iceberg itself was a rich, dark
blue you could almost mistake for an evening sky, were it not
for the fact that it dripped and creaked. Out through the French
windows I could see the open-air swimming pool. A camel swam
in its limpid waters. I advanced towards Jimmy and pressed the
banknotes into his trembling hands. "You dropped this," I said, and
turned to go.

"Wait," said Jimmy in a weak voice, and I stopped, and turned.
"One moment... I know it's here somewhere..." He opened a
wooden cabinet and rooted around in its interior. Was I finally
to be offered a glass of mead, in thanks for my kind deed? Jimmy
O'Bliss emerged with a bolt-action rifle.

"You're too fucking dangerous to live, Sonny Jim," he said,
cocking the gun with a snap of the bolt. A tremor ran through
the cliff of ice overhanging us, rattling the glass roof in its frame.
A little avalanche of slush and melt-water ran across the glass,
rippling the blue light that filtered through to us so that we
seemed to move underwater. "It is a thing I never understood,

in the James Bond fillums," said Jimmy O'Bliss, "why it is they always explain their nefarious plans to James Bond, and then leave him to be killed by some complicated, untried, and unsupervised stratagem. Lasers, indeed. Volcanoes. Fecking alligators… Myself and Charlie would always be roaring at the telly, 'Shoot him in the head! Just shoot him in the head!'" He sighed, pointed the gun at my head and pulled the trigger. The loud click of the firing pin on the empty chamber caused the cliff of ice above us to rumble, and lurch forward some inches. "Feck. No bullets. Hang on." He found a box of bullets in the cabinet.

"You are planning to shoot me in the head?" I said, somewhat taken aback.

"I am," he said, sliding out the empty magazine and loading it swiftly with bullets.

"That thought is a source of sorrow to me," I said, "for I am on a quest to win the heart of my true love, the most beautiful woman in Ireland and possibly the world."

"You intrigue me strangely," said Jimmy O'Bliss, pausing. "Tell me more."

I told him more.

"Sounds great. Where does she work?"

"In SuperMacs of Eyre Square, though currently, I believe, in the Hospital Canteen,."

He nodded, and closed his eyes, and smiled. "Ah, young love." He opened his eyes. "God, I haven't ridden the hole off a young one in a long while. Yes, I have neglected the needs of the Heart." He slammed the full magazine up into the gut of the gun with the palm of his hand. The tremendous blue ice-cliff overhanging us swayed and dropped a foot at the report. "Ah," he sighed, "youth is wasted on the young." He swung up the barrel.

"I was intrigued by the tunnel mouth," I said.

"What?" said Jimmy.

"Mr Bunne said something, too, about workers…"

"Oh, Big Mouth Strikes Again," said Jimmy. He put aside his

rifle. "Sure, I suppose it won't do any harm... This is where the Blacks are brought in. Hy Brasil is, by a curiosity of the law, in extra-territorial waters. Then down the tunnels with them, and Barney writes the cheque..."

I was puzzled. "Is such importation of shackled humanity strictly legal?"

"Our once and future King can do whatever he fucking wants here, sonny boy. It's his rocky kingdom, the barren field of his exile. From this stony grey soil he shall gather his strength, till the people repent their treachery and call for him..." Jimmy sighed. "He dragged this shit-hole out of the Middle Ages and into the twentieth fucking century, and how did the people thank him? They shafted him." He brooded a bit on this, and clarified. "They fucked him up the arse and hung him out to dry. But why am I still yapping? Old age..." He snapped up the bolt on the rifle, hauled it back, baring the chamber into which popped up, spring-loaded, a large bullet. He then slammed forward the bolt, knocking the bullet into position.

The cliff of ice above and behind him shifted, shifted again, lurched, and fell in its entirety on the banqueting hall, driving its stout pillars down through the next two floors, collapsing its own great wooden floor, the ancient carpet ripping free and sliding down the hole, so that I fell through the cellar, into the sub-cellar and rolled down the mouth of the tunnel wrapped in sheet and carpet. Jimmy, his suit snagging on a splintered joist as he fell through the cellar, did not follow me down. His rifle, jerked from his hands by his sudden arrest, did.

Now I had a gun. Jimmy did not. My position had improved.

Unfortunately, the collapsing iceberg had also breached the side wall of the open-air swimming pool, in which a camel still swam, alongside the banqueting hall.

It would have gone easier with me if the swimming pool had not been connected by a deep channel to the sea, to ensure the freshness of the bathing water: but it was: and the tide, too, being high, all the broad Atlantic attempted to follow me, camel and all, into the cellar, the sub-cellar, and, subsequently, the Tunnel.

32.

I fought free of the carpet, and surfaced, gasping, alongside the terrified camel. The wall of water was propelling us along the underground tunnel at astonishing speed, towards a pair of closed and sturdy metal doors. But, rather in the manner of a liquid Piston, the advancing water compressed the air ahead of it against the doors. The compressed air lifted them off their hinges long before the water itself arrived.

My ears sang as the air pressure collapsed. Then, as the wave began to approach the next set of metal doors, the pressure rose again...

My ears rang like bells after a couple of these pressure changes, and, tumbling in the turbulent front-waters of the advancing wave, I had trouble avoiding inhaling seawater, tangled as I was in my sheet, the strap of the heavy gun nearly pulling me under.

My chief concern, however, was to avoid the flailing hooves of the wild-eyed racing camel alongside me in the torrent, for if he were to tread me beneath the water I was a dead man.

I grasped the scruff of his neck. Taking a deep breath, I hauled myself aboard his great, stinking dun frame, up out of the stinking, roaring water. Though terrified, and bucking his mad head as we flew down the fluorescent corridor, his powerful legs seemed well able to keep him upright, high in the water and pointed in the right direction.

As I leaned forward to grasp his neck tighter, I felt a sharp stab in the thigh. I reached down and found a carpet tack caught in my sheet of Egyptian cotton. I pulled it loose, and fashioned it into a pin or clasp to hold my sheet about me as a kind of robe, freeing my hands to clutch his mane.

At length, the laws of fluid dynamics caused the flood to lose vigour, and the level and speed of it dropped to the point where the camel's thrashing hooves on occasion clipped solid ground.

We passed an open side-corridor, which diverted some of the flow, reducing our speed again, and I seized my moment.

Digging my heels into his flanks, I gave a great ululating cry. Noble racing beast that he was, he pinned back his ears, stretched forward his proud neck and swam as though his life depended upon it. Under the circumstances, I thought this wise. Bursting free of the wall of water with a great clatter of cloven hooves, he gave a snorting, bellowing roar of exultation.

I clung to the ochre mane of the mighty animal as he found his racing stride and pulled smoothly away from the great tide of debris and water pursuing us down the immigrant tunnel. Fluorescent lights flashed brightly and died above us, then ahead of us, as electrical equipment exploded and sparked and died beneath the chasing water.

At last we were in darkness, as our hoof-beats echoed their own echoes. Automatic doors swung open ahead of us, as we powered toward the light at the end of the tunnel.

We burst into the great Cavern of the Black Unit.

33.

My camel, confronted by a thousand toiling workers, bright lights, lasers, the noise of machinery, and the unexpected vastness of the space, slid to a halt on the smooth concrete floor. The door banged shut behind us. He reared, and pawed the air with his front hooves.

The .303 rifle of Jimmy O'Bliss, the strap of which I had entirely forgotten, slipped from my shoulder and I grabbed at the falling gun with quick, unthinking, reflexive fingers, one of which looped into the trigger-guard, causing the chambered bullet to discharge into the ceiling.

A thousand turned, and ceased their labour.

I adjusted the carpet tack holding my robe, and cleared my throat.

Murmurous cries went up.

"It is the spirit of Muhammad!"

"It is the spirit of Lenin!"

"It is the spirit of Zapata!"

"It is the spirit of Revolution, disguised, for reasons mysterious, as Lawrence of Arabia!"

"Our Liberator, at any rate! Come to free us!"

Several Workers took off their hairnets, threw them to the ground, and Danced upon them.

"There is a Great Wave coming!" I cried.

"Yes!" they cried, "The Revolution!"

"It will sweep away everything in its path!" I warned.

"Yes!"

"Allah akhbar!"

"Smash the system!"

"Overthrow the oppressors!"

"Follow me!" I cried.

"Yes!" they cried back.

"To Higher Ground!" I cried.

"We shall build the New Jerusalem thereupon," they cried. "The Workers' Paradise! Here on Earth!"

Some now began to sing the inspirational songs of Mr. Stevie Wonder, the blind visionary. Others sang the revolutionary songs of the group Public Enemy. Yet more sang the nihilistic yet vigorous songs of the Los Angeles collective Niggaz With Attitude, in particular their Fuck Tha Police, a tune which had always been very popular in the Orphanage. The younger workers then launched a cappella into Ain't No Nigga by Mr. Jay Z. Some sort of dispute then broke out between the singers, as to which of them was keeping it more real.

I noticed a familiar face across the crowded floor.

Babette was wrestling energetically with her father.

My nose tingled.

Digging my heels into my camel's flanks, I made my way through the crowd of cheering, singing, rapping workers to her side.

"Babette!" cried her father, breathing heavily, "What madness is this?"

"It is the Revolution of which I have secretly dreamed, Father!" said Babette. "And I throw in my lot with the Workers."

"All the flaws of your damned mother emerge!" said Barney O'Reilly Fitzpatrick McGee.

"Unhand the Ring," said Babette, and I saw that they wrestled for possession of a glowing ring of the stuff which I had inadvertently ignited on my previous visit.

"Can I be of assistance?" I said to Babette.

"Smite my father," said Babette.

I smote him.

He fell, smitten.

"Take my hand," said Babette.

I took her hand, and she pulled herself up on to the camel.

"Hurrah!" the cries went up.

"He has smitten the tyrant!"

"He has chosen his bride!"

"He resembles the young Leonardo DiCaprio!"

"The daughter of the tyrant has joined the revolution!"

The crowd quietened. There was a sound of murmuring Workers. Then even the murmurs ceased.

The crowd looked at me.

I looked at the crowd.

Nobody was moving towards the stairs, lifts, or Emergency Exits.

I was beginning to think that I had been in some way misinterpreted.

"I loved your metaphor of the Great Wave," said Babette, looking back over her shoulder at me. There was definitely something about her face, or perhaps her smell, or even the way she now nuzzled her perfect buttocks back against my crotch... "The Great Wave..." she murmured. "A magnificent, powerful image."

The tunnel doors softly opened, and papers blew gently from the nearby desks in a little breeze.

"I'm afraid my Rhetorical Skills cannot take full credit for that one," I said, as a Wall of Water exploded through the open doors of the great cavern.

34.

I rode for the Emergency Stairwell.

"Follow Lawrence!" "Follow Lenin!" "Muhammad!" "Zapata!" "Our Liberator!" cried a thousand voices, "The forces of Reaction are Swift!" "They may kill us but they can never kill the spirit of the Revolution!"

As the torrent of Atlantic seawater covered the floor of the Black Unit's Cavern and began to rise, I found myself clattering up the Emergency Stairwell at the head of a great mass of revolting Workers.

The Jogging action involved in riding a racing camel up a lengthy flight of stairs thrust Babette's buttocks repeatedly against my trouser front. This caused a significant lengthening of my Original Organ. The lack of fly-buttons on my Charity Suit allowed it to advance from the shelter of my trousers. Her skirt and my sheet having both ridden up, my organ was soon lodged between the golden orbs of her proud revolutionary rear.

Further advance was impeded only by Panties scarcely worthy of the name, being little more than a strip of silk running from tailbone to bellybutton through her Golden Vale.

We emerged from the stairwell at the head of a ragged army and stormed across the entrance lobby of Westcom and out through the automatic doors, into the Car Park.

"Have you ever read the book Wuthering Heights?" she said over her shoulder.

"I have not," I replied.

"Or seen the black and white film Wuthering Heights?"

"I have not."

"Or the inferior colour remake?"

"No."

"A pity," she sighed, and, reaching back with her right hand, hooked a finger in the silken strip and pulled the last cobweb of an obstacle away.

With an upward tilt of her behind, a wriggle, and a push, she caused my organ to slide between the warm, welcoming lips of her labia, juicy from the various stimulations of our camel-ride. Her heaped skirts and my great sheet, piled over my thighs, obscured our love-making from the others.

"I have waited many years for this glorious Day!" cried an ecstatic old man, his face black, his hair white, running alongside me.

"Indeed, so have I," I replied. The Organ Practice of the Girls behind Frankie's Arcade was a rough thing in comparison with this.

"Faster! Faster!" cried Babette, rocking her pelvis back and forth. Her tailbone rotated about my pubic bone in such a manner as to excite a further extension of my considerably extended organ. "Yes! Yes!" she cried, as indeed did I also. "Yes! Yes! Oh, faster! Yes! Yes!"

I became dimly aware of a thousand voices crying "Yes! Yes!" in rhythm with my Thrusting. Looking about me, I realised that both Camel and Mob had believed Babette and I to be addressing them. As a consequence, we had all of us advanced at a considerable speed into Galway City. Indeed, we had crossed half the City and were halfway up Mill Street.

The sight of a man and woman energetically riding a camel at the head of a ragged but enthusiastic company of Non-Nationals appeared to throw the Natives of Galway into confusion. Small children hid behind their mothers in doorways. Grown men leapt over garden walls for safety. Indeed, so great was the uproar that a guard actually appeared at the door of Mill Street Garda Station.

"Yes! Yes! Faster! Faster!" cried the Workers, who were by now sprinting to keep up with our racing camel. "Lead us, Lawrence!"

"Lenin!"

"Muhammad!"

"Zapata!"

"We will follow you to the ends of the earth!"

I pulled up the camel outside the Police Station. I intended to disabuse my followers of the notion that I knew where I was going.

"Friends!" I cried. They roared their approval.

"Don't stop!" cried Babette, her eyes closed, her tender interior beginning to contract about my Organ.

"We shall never stop!" they roared. "Until we have built..."

"...Heaven!..." cried Babette.

"...On Earth!" cried the Workers.

"Oh Jesus and Maria!" cried Babette, and began to convulse atop the camel, her Contractions of Pleasure nearly removing my penis at the root. "Oh! Oh! Oh God, I'm dying! Oh!"

"The Filthy Police have shot our Leader's Beloved!" cried the crowd, and stormed Mill Street Police Station, raiding its armoury before burning it to the ground.

35.

While the Mob were engaged in burning down the Police Station, I attempted to sneak away. I found Sneaking, however, surprisingly difficult atop a racing camel with my tumescent Organ held tight in the warm embrace of a lady's intimate parts. Babette seemed reluctant for me to leave, and indeed I found myself strangely reluctant to leave her.

Thus it was that I urged the camel into a gentle trot, away from the burning Police Station. The unfortunate upshot of this gentle trot was the renewal of our old rhythm and a loss of concentration on my part.

By the time we were passing the Army Barracks at Renmore, my Organ was on the Brink of an Immense Event unprecedented in my Erotic History. I plunged at every step into the deepest depths of a Babette whose beauty grew ever more clear to me.

Opening my eyes, I looked around me, and was appalled to discover all my Sneaking had been in Vain: A thousand Revolutionary Workers, and some Bohermore Lads, were trotting at my heels.

From the watchtower at the gate of Renmore Barracks two soldiers Watched us.

"I don't think much of this year's Parade," said one loudly to the other. "He doesn't look like Saint Patrick at all."

"I think he's meant to be Santa Claus," said the other.

In turning my head, I brushed my now enormous Nose against the long hair of Babette. She turned to investigate, and, struck by my nose's striking resemblance to a virile male member, and made lascivious by the movement of my original Organ deep within her, licked the length of my erectile nose from root to tip.

"Nah, he's Rudolph the Red-Nosed Reindeer."

I missed the rest of their remarks as I was preoccupied with experiencing the most astonishing Orgasm of my young life.

Both my Members throbbed in unison, both now so filled with my heart's blood that I nearly fainted for lack of it elsewhere.

I threw back my head and ululated in ecstasy, dislodging the Carpet Tack that had held my makeshift robe in place. It fell between myself and Babette, as I rocked backward in my pleasure-spasm, and was lost to sight. Rocking forward again, I found it.

Unable to stop my Orgasmic Rhythm, yet driving a carpet-tack deeper into my right upper thigh, or lower buttock, with every thrust, I emitted cries of pain indistinguishable from pleasure and cries of pleasure that could not be told apart from those of pain.

Certainly my followers could not distinguish them, for they cried "The Filthy Soldiers have machine-gunned our Beloved Leader!"

Having seen the havoc caused by their previous misunder-standing, and fearing they would Storm and Burn the Barracks, I endeavoured, in my weak, post-coital state, to explain to them the cause of my anguished cries. I pulled the source of my discomfort from my Buttock. This was achieved with difficulty, for the tack had left little protruding, and my hands had frozen into almost useless fists after so long spent tightly clutching for dear life the mane of a camel. I held it in my raised fist and shook it to attract their attention. They hesitated an instant, looking to me for Leadership, Guidance, and a Calming of their Bloodlust.

"Speak to us!" cried the Workers. "What are the last, sacred orders of our great Dying Leader?"

Suspecting that errors in communication had led to the last Arson, I decided to make my explanation as simple as possible. Waving my fist in the air, I cried:

"A Tack! A Tack!"

They stormed the Renmore Barracks, raiding its armoury before burning it to the ground.

36.

I took what lessons I could from the experience, and led my heavily-armed people onward. Somewhat drained, I fell into a light sleep.

When I awoke, the smoking Barracks had been left behind. We had halted. Our path was blocked by a great gate. Afraid of unleashing the wrath of the workers, I made no sudden gestures.

I surveyed the heavy gates, the high walls topped with spiked fence and razor wire, the low, reinforced concrete guardhouse.

"What dreadful prison is this?" I whispered in Babette's delicate ear.

"No prison," she said, turning, a slow smile coming upon her face that caused my heart to pound. "We stand at the gates of the estate of the young urban professionals. We have found our earthly paradise."

Miguel de Navarra stepped from the guardhouse with tears in his eyes. "Liberador! El Nuevo Zapata! Mi caro!" he cried.

The gates glided silently apart, and we entered Paradise.

37.

How beautiful it was. The grounds were artfully landscaped, being built on seven artificial hillocks. A charming stream wound round the little hills. The great houses lay silent, scattered, half hidden in the vast grounds.

Babette and I dismounted and walked the grounds together hand-in-hand. Miguel showed us the sights.

"And where," I said at length, "are the young urban professionals?" I was eager to see one, for though I had heard of them, they were a species unknown in Tipperary.

"Oh they're never here. They are all out working all hours to pay their enormous Mortgages."

"What is a Mortgage?"

"It is a word from the French, or rather Norman," said Babette softly, "describing a type of bank loan used to buy property: *Mort*, meaning dead, and *Gage*, meaning hand. Thus a mortgage is a dead hand upon the property."

"That is a most informative explanation."

"Thank you. I love your cock."

I surveyed the beautiful rolling acres of unpopulated greensward. Not a body, not a voice, not a toy. I asked Miguel, "But are there no Children, nor the minders of Children?"

"The Bourgeois Oppressors of the Poor cannot afford to Breed, nor have they the time or energy, for they are too Wealthy and Successful," he said.

We made free with the canned foodstuffs of the Oppressor, and had a revolutionary picnic, for we were starving. The Workers drew lots for their quarters and moved in, removing the bourgeois locks from the revolutionary doors.

And then began an idyll.

38.

That first evening, after the revolutionary picnic, Babette and I went for a lovely walk around the estate, inside the great Security Wall and Gates.

Then we went for a lovely walk around the estate, outside the great Security Wall and Gates.

Upon finishing our Walks, Babette suggested a number of possible improvements to the Grounds and Surrounds. "That all sounds Lovely," I said, looking into her glorious green eyes a-glow in the umber sunset. At once the large number of young men who had been following us gave a great revolutionary Shout, and dispersed in small groups.

They began dynamiting nearby derelict buildings, felling trees which obscured our fine views of the nearby slums, digging great earthen embankments inside the walls and constructing a magnificent network of earthworks, trenches, slopes, and tunnels.

I was awoken from our Kissing by the warm summery gust of a nearby combustion of dynamite.

"Will the residents not object?" I said, as one of the buildings within the estate slowly collapsed like a shot Elephant.

"It impeded our field of fire," whispered Babette, nibbling my ear.

"Oh, fair enough," I said.

"Besides," she said, "They don't own the estate anymore."

"That's OK then, so," I said.

"It has been appropriated by the People."

"Are we the people?" I asked.

"We are," she replied.

"Well, that's a bit of luck," I said.

A roofing-tile whizzed past.

We kissed.

39.

And so the idyll continued, all through the long summer.

We planted maíz and recreational plants in the traditional manner on the terraces and extensive patios of the great estate houses. We adapted the fountains and water-features to irrigate the growing crop.

On the south facing balconies we hung wet towels of thick cotton, and grew watercress and mustard upon them. We took siestas in the heat of the afternoon. In the evening the younger software engineers put on revolutionary dramas.

At night we all contributed our suggestions for the Revolutionary Website, and voted on the next day's plans.

Sometimes Babette would address us.

"Who must we study, brothers? From whom can we learn?" she cried. "Marx, Brothers!"

The workers cheered, and I nodded. Though I had heard of the Marx Brothers, I was somewhat handicapped by never having seen their Vaudeville show or their famous moving pictures. However, I was familiar with the photograph of the eldest brother on the cover of *The Collected Letters of Groucho Marx*. It had been one of the most popular books in the orphanage library until Brother Ormond had burned it in error during one of his purges. If I ever found another copy of the book, I vowed silently to study it.

The summer days drifted endlessly by.

Occasionally a half-hearted Army patrol would approach the walls and we would mobilise the field-workers. "Don't mind us," the Army would shout. "Only, the Americans asked us to ask ye, are ye Communists?"

"No!" we shouted.

"Socialists?"

"No!" we said, less loudly.

"Anarchists?"

"No," we mumbled awkwardly, after a bit of a pause.

"Sorry, I missed that," replied the patrol.

"Not really!" we shouted.

"That's great lads, thanks!" shouted the Irish Army, and sped off.

In time, many of their Soldiers joined us.

The first of the children were born in the Spring.

40.

I tilled the fields an hour or two a day; I helped my Comrades prepare meals from the harvest of the garden; I indulged in leisurely evening discourse with the community as we planned a heaven of equality and freedom here on earth; and I made love with Babette every night till dawn, and again on awaking, usually rising from bed in time for a hearty breakfast well before noon.

My dissatisfaction grew.

One evening, Babette turned to me in bed. She slid aside from her lap the sleek Apple Computer on which she had been designing the Revolutionary Website, and ran her sensitive fingers across my brow. "There is something wrong."

"Yes," I said.

"There is something missing in your life."

"Yes," I said. "My first love haunts me yet. I thought I had gotten over her. I have not. I yearn to accomplish the task she set me, and win her heart. But a drawback of living in a Socialist Paradise is that it is difficult to earn a million pounds. Above all, perhaps, I yearn to see her face, to speak little words of love, to bid her wait for me to grow worthy of her love..."

Silently, Babette passed me the Apple, and bowed low her head. Some time passed.

"You are perhaps hinting at something?" I hazarded.

She sighed, and rubbed the tears from her chin with the back of her hand. She pressed some computer buttons for me. "It is CIA searchware," she said. "We bought it off the Bohermore lads. Type in her name, and anything you know of her, in the various boxes."

"Boxes?"

"I shall guide your hand."

My finger hovered. I realised I did not know her name.

I hit the letters with my finger, my tongue held loosely

between my front teeth to steady me.

"Female," I typed. Babette guided me, by whisper and touch. With another finger I typed "SuperMacs, Eyre Square, Galway" and "The Canteen, The Hospital, Galway" as last known places of employment.

Babette poked a button.

The screen went blank for some time. At length it said "Subject Not Found". I sighed. The Salmon leapt in the breast pocket of my pyjamas.

A name appeared upon the screen.

Angela

The name of my first love.

"Angela," I murmured.

And then:

Patient number 47/3901/Q. Ward Seven, The Merciful Hour Lunatic Asylum, Northside, Dublin
-*Department of Health and Social Welfare, record of clients, Eastern Health Board.*

And then:

Physics tries to discover the pattern of events which controls the phenomena we observe. But we can never know what this pattern means or how it originates; and even if some superior intelligence were to tell us, we should find the explanation unintelligible.
-*Sir James Hopwood Jeans, English scientist, Physics and Philosophy, 1942.*

I sighed a deep sigh. Babette took back the Apple. She did not look at my first love's name, and address. She pressed the Apple's halves back together with a sigh, and with a sigh it slept. She put away the Apple, and put her hand on mine. I drew her to me. We made love till dawn.

Eventually, exhausted, Babette slept.

I lay awake a while, troubled by my new knowledge. Finally I fell asleep, beside the sleeping woman and the Apple.

When we awoke, Babettte helped me pack my black bag. We slipped out of the security gates.

She walked me to the station in the rain.

41.

At the station I walked away, down the deserted platform.

Babette called me back. I halted. She came up and gave me a Novelty Lunchbox, in the shape of an Accordion, in Pleated Plastic. She opened the lid as I held it in my hands. A hidden device began to play *The Fields of Athenry*, in small, cheerful, single notes. I peered within to see a Bar of Chocolate and three large mustard and watercress sandwiches masking the mechanism.

I looked into her eyes and she into mine. At length the silence seemed to call with unusual urgency for words. I cleared my throat and her bright eyes brightened.

"It is a lovely Novelty Lunchbox," I said.

She nodded.

I turned.

She called me back.

I halted.

She came up and produced something from a pocket of her revolutionary blouse.

The Ring.

Softly warmly glowing. She held it out to me and I took it from her hand. The warm and tiny ring. The gesture seemed filled with symbolic significance. "It is a lovely ring," I said.

She nodded. The tears dripped from her chin.

"Thank you," I said.

She nodded. She opened her mouth. She closed her mouth.

"Can I do anything for you in return," I said.

She shrugged. "Oh, you know." She opened her mouth. She closed her mouth. "Whatever. Slay me a dragon. The usual." She turned and walked away.

"I shall do my best," I said, but I do not think she heard me.

I walked the length of the platform, past the silent, empty train.

"Jude..." cried Babette from behind me.

"Yes?" I answered, turning.

"Why don't you just stick it... stick it... shove it, in your... navel, why don't you?" she shouted, and turned, and ran sobbing from the station.

Puzzled, I stuck it in my navel, settling it in carefully so that it disappeared entirely. Its warm glow was pleasant. Then I descended the steps at the end of the platform. I stepped with a crunch onto the loose limestone rubble on which lay the wooden sleepers and the steel tracks. I stepped sideways over the nearside track, and kept walking in long strides, from wooden sleeper to wooden sleeper, away from Ceannt Station, and Galway, and Babette. Once, I looked back.

Babette had gone.

I turned, and walked on.

42.

The walk to Dublin was pleasant, and passed through fine country. As I strode through Athenry, I waved cheerily at the farmers assembled on the station platform. Some raised their Hats.

Once I had left the perpetual rain of County Galway behind me, the weather was bright and clear, and I began to make good time.

Occasionally I would lie on the south-facing bank, and rest in the weak sun. A surprise to me were the extraordinary numbers of apple-trees growing, straggling and wild, up both banks alongside the tracks. Indeed, for much of the journey, I seemed to be walking along a path cut through an abandoned orchard two hundred miles long.

I eked out my watercress and mustard sandwiches with wizened autumn apples from the trees. I was saving the bar of chocolate to celebrate my safe arrival in our Capital City, and to give me energy for the ordeals I would no doubt have to endure there, in the search for my True Love.

Several times a day, I would hear a train coming. I would make my way up the bank to safety, and watch it pass. Once, a passenger hurled an apple core from a window as the train flew by. The core landed high on the wild bank, near me, and that solved the mystery of the long orchard.

But I preferred the nights, when there were no trains.

At night the steel tracks glinted bright in the small light of a filling moon, and my steady tread from sleeper to sleeper slowly altered my consciousness. The repetition of identically measured steps, and the unchanging view down the miles of straight track, built up a colossal reservoir of identical memories into which I sank as it grew deeper and deeper. My memory of a second ago was identical to my memory of an hour ago, was identical to my memory of this instant. And I lost my habitual sense that time had a velocity, and a direction, and applied to me. Imperceptibly I grew certain that, beyond question, the next instant would be identical to this one: and so it was. And I grew certain that, in an hour's time, I would be experiencing an instant identical to this, to that, to those: and so it came to be, with less and less sense of anything coming to be.

The sky, eventually, changed colour, but not fast enough to replace the illusion of timelessness with the illusion of time.

So pleasant was this endless moment that I grew disturbed by the occasional appearance of Towns, which drifted toward me with an unsettling degree of movement and change. Also, I did not greatly enjoy the rain of small stones, oaths and phlegm which accompanied my passage through the urban areas of the midlands. Thus I took to walking through the Towns with my eyes closed, the stones bouncing harmlessly off my head, only reopening my eyes when I could again hear birdsong and the lowing of cattle.

But, eventually, I found I had been walking with my eyes closed for far longer than usual, and still I heard no cattle. This town was surely a mighty town. Could I have entered the outskirts of Dublin City itself?

I opened my eyes.

43.

It was indeed the approach to Dublin City.

I was soon so lost in wonder that I forgot to strip the golden foil off my bar of chocolate before eating it.

My Track now ran alongside another Track, for Dublin was so vast a city, its public infrastructure so prodigal after a decade of Economic Plenty, that a train could enter it and a train leave it at the same time.

Tall, spiked fences topped the high banks to either side of this broad avenue, and kept stray animals and men away from the tracks. I enjoyed the luxury of being out of range of rock and phlegm. Dizzy with the sweetness of the rich chocolate, exultant with triumph, spitting gold foil, I luxuriated in the Approach to the Capital.

The famed barbed wire of Dublin began to appear, topping the spiked fences. At first single strands, then multiple strands, then great bundles, bushes, clouds of barbed wire, double barbs, razor wire, topping fences which were not just spiked but bent out and electrified. Fences gave way to walls. Some wall-tops glittered with broken glass, sparkling green, white and orange in the lowering sun. Some walls were topped with gay rows of playful rotating spikes. But above, around, upon it all: barbed wire. Barbed wire upon the broken glass, entwining the rotating spikes, winding up the drainpipes and running wild along the gutters. So much barbed wire! There was not a farm in Tipperary could compete with the bounty of Dublin. Here, the humblest home, factory or shed was bedecked and garlanded with a quantity of wire that you would scarcely see the match of across fifty acres of family farm in Tipperary's Golden Vale. I knew well the price of good quality galvanised double-barb wire, and I was over-awed, indeed almost frightened, by the ostentatious wealth on display as we entered Dublin proper. I had had no idea the Capital of my Nation suffered so greatly from the problem of stray cattle. Indeed, dear God, what quantity of cattle did such a quantity of barbed wire portend!

The tracks split, and split again, and in an orgy of infrastructure entered Heuston Station. I walked among the trains in the great Shed, past the buffers that ended my empty Galway track, and hopped up on the platform. I made my way through the crowd attempting to fight their way onto the Cork train, and the crowd trying to fight their way off the Limerick train, and crossed the foyer.

Emerging from Heuston station, I was astonished to find Dublin was not knee-deep in cowshit.

"Have you any idea where the Lunatic Asylum is?" I asked a fleeing Tourist.

He pointed across the river at North Dublin. "The whole

120

fucking place is a lunatic asylum," he said, and disappeared into Heuston station at a limping trot.

Reassured that I was headed in the right direction, I crossed the Liffey, and entered the historic North Side of Dublin City.

DUBLIN

44.

Above and around me soared the magnificent tiny houses and occasional blocks of flats for which the Northside of Dublin was famed. Dear dirty Dublin! The open spaces between the flats were full of the vibrant life of a tight-knit community which had remained unchanged for a thousand years, apart from the massacre of its original inhabitants by the Vikings; the decline and defeat of the Viking settlers in the eleventh century; the crushing of both Celt and Viking remnant by the Norman foe in the thirteenth century; the inter-tribal warfare, betrayals, and collapse of Brehon Law; the decline, isolation and stagnation of the Middle Ages; the utter devastation, rape, slaughter and population displacement of the Elizabethan plantations of the sixteenth century; the brutal oppression, sectarian massacres and decline under Cromwell; the annihilation of the Irish language and suppression of Irish Catholicism under the Penal Laws; the devastation of the 1798 rising, the decline of Dublin after the illegal abolition of Grattan's Parliament and the bribed passage of the Act of Union in 1801; the brutal crushing of the 1803 rising; the malnutrition, population displacement, emigration, immigration, mass deaths and social disruption of the Famine from 1845-1851; the brutal crushing of the small 1848 rising, the brutal crushing of the large 1867 rising; further population displacement and social havoc wrought by the delayed and partial Irish Industrial Revolution; the subsequent demolition of the old slums and replacement by new slums; the massacre of volunteer manhood in World War One, the shelling of the city by British gunboats and the massacre of civilians and volunteer manhood in the rising of 1916; the slaughter and devastation of the war of independence; the economic stagnation and emigration following independence; the betrayals and devastation of the civil war; the social and economic devastation of the abolition and destruction of the brothel district in 1925; the total economic implosion of the Economic War against England under de Valera; the economic collapse and massacre of volunteer manhood in World War Two, the economic stagnation and emigration following World War Two, the economic stagnation and emigration of the 1950s, the economic stagnation and emigration of the 1960s; the demolition of the new slums and replacement by yet newer slums of the 1970s; the economic stagnation, emigration and devastation of the heroin epidemic of the 1980s; and the heroin, crime, economic stagnation, paramilitary racketeering and violence, social collapse, emigration, immigration, drug gang warfare, betrayal by successive governments and soaring property prices of the 1990s.

Dear dirty Dublin, entirely unchanged.

45.

A familiar figure emerged from a slum doorway, a brown envelope in his hand. Jimmy O'Bliss. Our nation's greatest developer, his selfless labours never ceasing. He knew every brick in the city, having put half of them there himself.

He limped swiftly away. Yes, I would ask his directions to the Asylum. I hurried after. He sped up.

I sped up.

He sped up again.

Some time later, I looked all about me.

No human figures stirred. The great open spaces, surrounded by piles of concrete and rubble to stop the Travellers from halting here, were silent. A rectangle of printed paper drifted down past me, then another, a handful, a blizzard of pieces of paper… A gust of wind lifted them, sent them soaring back up. I seized one from the air, and studied it.

"**Parking Ticket**," it said, followed by a number of smaller words. I let it go. The small storm of parking tickets fluttered down about me again, and were seized by another gust and thrust upward, in the circulating currents between the towers.

I looked up. The balconies of the flats were deserted. Only towels and underclothes moved gently there. Of whom could I request directions?

The ground-floor door of the nearest flat opened. A young man in a Manchester United replica shirt walked outside, closed his door, took out his longfellow, and began to urinate high upon his own front door.

I cleared my throat.

"What are *you* looking at?" he said in a Dublin accent of great strength and localness.

"I'm sorry, my curiosity was aroused by the fact that you seem to be pissing upon your own front door."

The young man turned, spat in my general direction, and began to lower his trousers and under-shorts.

"Eh? Mine? No. I live *inside*. The *outside* of the door is the council's responsibility. And the step. *Council's*. Council owns it."

"I see."

He squatted, strained briefly, and deposited a long coil of

125

excrement on his door-step.

Seizing a passing Parking Ticket, he wiped his sphincter, then stood and pulled up his pants.

He opened his door to re-enter his home. The puddle of his piss had spread under the door to soak into the rotting edge of the carpet. "Gah!" he said, and, distracted, trod in his own shit. "Tsk! Look at the state of this step! Council do nothing for us round here! Nothing for us decent, salt-of-the-Earth Dubs! Too busy giving money and mobiles and Mercs and mansions to the Niggers!" I scratched my head, as he continued, "The Blacks get everything and we get fuck all!"

"But you yourself," I pointed out, "are a black man."

He took a squelching step toward me and drew back his fist. I bent to pick up one of the severed wing mirrors which lay in the gutter, noticing in the process that I had picked up quite a tan myself, no doubt from working in the commune's fields, and from my long walk. I held the mirror up to his face. His fist fell to his side. He stared into the mirror and began to breathe heavily.

"Dear God! Dear Jesus! The rumours were true! My Dada a Black Man! My Mam a Nigger-Lover! And I... a Nigger! A Nigger! In my House! There will be no Nigger in my House!"

And with a great shout and his arms about his own shoulders he got his head in a headlock and threw himself out of his flat.

"Cyril, are you all right there, man?" came a cry from a balcony above.

"There was a Nigger in my House!" cried Cyril, bending his left arm behind his back and wrenching it painfully high with his right.

"Jesus! I'll get the Lads! We'll be right down!"

"Oh, I have him! He's going nowhere!" said Cyril, and hauled up hard on his left wrist with his right hand.

The Lads arrived.

"I'll hold him down, you hit him," said Cyril and, throwing himself violently to the ground, released his left wrist briefly in order to grab himself by the scruff of the neck and bounce his face off the concrete. He resumed the arm-lock, as the lads began to methodically kick him about the head and upper body.

"What the *fuck* are you looking at, cuntface?" said one of the lads.

I smiled to indicate I meant him no harm.

"What are you, a fucking faggot?" said another.

"Check the fucking gold tooth, lads."

"Fucking foreigner, is it?"

"Fucking Romanian more like."

A number of the lads left off kicking Cyril's head to surround me.

"What the fuck are you doing here anyway, cunty?"

"Yeah."

"Yeah."

"Yeah."

I realised at once that they believed me to be a foreigner, and that they did not like foreigners. It must be the Gold Tooth! I tried to dislodge the foil of the chocolate wrapper from my front tooth with the tip of my tongue, but with no success.

"He's sticking his fucking tongue out at us!" cried a Lad. They all took a step towards me, frowning and rolling up the sleeves of their Ireland, Celtic, Leeds and Manchester United replica football shirts. I tried to dislodge the foil with my index finger.

"He's giving us the finger!" They took another step forward. One began to examine his baseball bat. Someone appeared to have driven nails into it. His frown deepened.

I gave up on the foil. The best course would simply be to clarify why I was passing through their neighbourhood, prove my Irishness, and thus put their minds at rest.

I smiled. I saw the flash of my gold tooth in my dark face reflected in their eyes, which now moved closer.

"I seek the Asylum," I said, but they did not seem to hear me clearly, for they spat on their hands and one swung his spiked bat

and they advanced on me, as I dropped my plastic accordion and
shouted again, my Gold Tooth flashing again in the sun, "I seek
the Asylum! I seek the Asylum! Please help me to find the Asylum
I seek!"

46.

They pursued me across rough ground for some considerable
time.

47.

Eventually my pursuers were distracted by a small Welshman
emerging from a Launderette. As they beat him unconscious with
a long piece of two-by-four, I succeeded in putting good distance
between us.

With them far behind me, I slowed to a brisk walk. A colossal
grey stone building lay ahead of me. On the small sign by its open
gate were the words 'The North Dublin Merciful Hour Lunatic
Asylum'. Oh happy accident! Walking up the long gravel path,
through the deserted gardens, I looked up at the myriad windows.
Some were closed, some open. Some barred, some unbarred.

None both open and unbarred.

A man stood on the steps, weeping. A familiar man.

Jimmy O'Bliss.

I joined him, on the steps.

"You!" he said, sobbing through his scarf. "You caused this
desolation! You led me to this sorrow! You!"

"How so?" I said, surprised.

"Did you not tell me of your Chip Shop Love?" said Jimmy

O'Bliss. "Did I not track her down and chat her up? Did I not ply her with cocaine and Courvoisier? Did I not, after weeks of wooing, get up on her and ride the hole off of her? Did I not lose my heart to the double-jointed slut? Did she not tip into psychosis after a three-day orgy of superior Amsterdam hydroponic skunkweed, unlimited uncut medical-quality cocaine and nine bottles of Very Special Old Pale, in the penthouse suite of the Clarence Hotel? Did I not have to commit her under section 172 of the Mental Treatment Act of 1945? Do I not now stand upon the steps of the Asylum weeping for all I have lost, unable to bring myself to visit her pale shell?" He paused to weep the more. "You did, I did, I did, I did, I did, she did, I did, and I do," he wept. "And it's all your fucking fault."

His sodden scarf slid down his face under its weight of tears, revealing a pale jaw and full lips moistened by the flowing tears.

"What are you going to do?" I said, after a respectful pause.

"What can I do?" he sobbed. "I'll contribute to the 'campaign expenses' of the Minister for Health, have 'a word' with the committee compiling the report on the future of mental health provision in Ireland, beat the next-nearest tender for the Merciful Hour by a grand through a suitable offshore front, get a change-of-use, funnel a bit of money through a 'consultant' to half the City Councillors plus one, they'll re-zone it, I'll knock it, and build a luxurious gated community whose penthouse apartments command magnificent views of this shit-hole of a city. But will that bring her back to me?" he sobbed. "It will not!"

Throwing his scarf back around his face, he pushed past me in his torment and ran through the grounds and out the gate, to vanish among the burnt-out cars.

I stood on the steps for a while longer, inhaling the misty, smoky, dusty air.

At length I came up with a most extraordinarily magnificent Plan. I tore off a strip of lining from my coat, and, wrapping it about my face, I walked up the steps and through the doors.

48.

I entered the spacious foyer and inhaled the beautiful, familiar odour of linoleum-polish. I had to shake my head in order to dislodge an image of myself in the Orphanage, and of the lost Long Corridor stretching away into darkness.

I approached the desk, behind which stood a man.

"I have come from Galway to see Angela," I said entirely truthfully through my ragged scarf.

"Ah," he said. "The legendary Jimmy O'Bliss! You are taller than I imagined. And younger. And your wig is much more convincing than I was led to believe."

I nodded. And I sighed. Already my morality grew more Sophisticated and Refined in the crucible of the city, and I had been here but an hour. I shook his hand.

"Pleased to meet you, Jimmy," he said.

"Please, Doctor," I said. "My friends call me Jude." Damn! A slip. But the man made nothing of it.

A corridor. A stairs, up. A corridor. A stairs, down. A corridor.

At length we arrived at a door.

I stared through the little window in the door. Time passed.

"Ah..." he said at last, "If there's anything... If I can..."

"I would like you to go away," I said.

The man in the suit went to go, and came back.

I looked at him, over the frayed rim of my scarf.

He went again as though to go, and came back. "Ah... Jimmy... can I call you Jimmy..."

"No," I said, in another slip.

"Sorry... Sorry... Mr. O'Bliss. You won't... Times change... I mean, God be with the days... But under the new guidelines, it

130

is no longer considered acceptable to rape the loonies... I know, I know... I mean, it's nothing to do with me, some sort of European law... Fecking bureaucrats in Brussels, ha ha... Obviously if it were up to me, grand..."

"That is not my intention," I said.

"Good... Good... OK, so... I'll be... I'll be just, in my office, so..."

He went.

I saw her through glass. The glass was reinforced with wire. The grid of wire within the glass made a grid of the room, of her, as though she had been carefully and perfectly painted, from a photograph, onto graph paper.

It reminded me of photographs I had seen of the Moon. Photographs taken, by the American Astronauts, with a kind of camera that put a grid of little crosses on each photograph in order to judge scale and distance and to fit them all together later. To make a map of the Moon.

She was very like the moon, so bright, so clear, so far away. Her pale face, her pale hair, floating. I could not breathe.

I could not breathe.

Her face seemed to fill my vision. Her lips and hair, her eyes, the profile of her nose, her chin. She turned to laugh at something I could not hear through the glass. With the turn of her head I felt a spasm in my heart. She slid the stub of her lipstick across the top lip, then the bottom.

Her lips glistened in the darkness.

I looked away, and breathed, and breathed, and breathed.

Eventually the man returned. I was still breathing.

"We must close," he said. "I'm sorry, I'm sorry."

I left, and they closed the asylum.

Using the Wellington Monument as my landmark, I made my way to the Phoenix Park. I climbed a tall oak trunk, until it branched. There, at the heart of the tree, was a broad, curved space as big as a bed, from around which the branches curved away and up. This great hollow had filled with fallen leaves, every year of the old century, leaves which had rotted to a compost in which grasses and small plants and flowers grew. This soft base was now covered with a thick duvet of this year's crisp, dry leaves. I burrowed deep under the crisp dry leaves, to lie among the feathered, desiccated skeletons of fledgling blue-tits and wrens which had fallen from their nests in the higher branches in the spring, as I had enjoyed my idyll in the Galway commune.

I closed my eyes and breathed, and breathed, and breathed.

Eventually I slept.

49.

I must have been tired, after days and nights of walking the railway tracks towards my true love with no sleep, for I slept among the skeletons, deep beneath the leaves, for all of the night and most of the next day.

When I made my way back to the Asylum, it was already almost dark. But there were no lights on in the locked windows, or in the unlocked windows, or in the barred windows, or in the unbarred. Dim figures in the dim light filled the grounds. I walked toward the dark Asylum through the murmuring crowd, covered my face, and then up the steps, and in the door…

The man stood up. He slid a large brown envelope with difficulty into his inside jacket pocket.

"I have come to visit Angela," I said, thinking, 'This time, I shall speak, I shall speak of love.'

The man laughed.

I frowned.

The man frowned. "Did I not tell you yesterday, Mr O'Bliss, that we had to close the Asylum? We have closed the Asylum.

It is closed."

"Closed?" I said.

The man gave me a big wink. In reflex I gave him a wink in return, and he relaxed and smiled. "The committee which I chair," said the man, smiling, "has reluctantly decided that the Merciful Hour has no place in the future of mental health provision in Ireland. No, the future lies in Care in the Community. A mysterious figure," said the man, with a wink, "has bought the place, had it re-zoned, and is about to knock it and build a luxurious gated community whose penthouse apartments will command magnificent views of... But I am wandering from the point." He ushered me to the door. "You will enjoy this... Of course, technically the building is protected so we'll have to work fast..." He cried from the top of the steps, "Get out! We're closed! Get out! Get out!"

Distant Machinery ground into life. Some great mechanical thing loomed up out of the fog. A wrecking ball swung in through a barred window on the top floor, sending sparks flying as the iron ball struck the flint sill and lintel, and the iron bars. Lumps of stone and rods of iron tumbled down the façade, and cascaded down the steps. Screams came from the dim crowd in the grounds.

"Get out!" He drove them before him, out the gate into the road. I followed, looking for Angela. The crowd milled, and murmured, and some shook the railings and the gate, trying to regain the Asylum. But another wrecking crew joined in, and another, and soon the roof fell in, blasting jets of dust out of every shattered window, floor by floor, all the way down.

The crowd sighed, and cried, and turned, and began to drift away.

I had not found her, in the panicky dark, in the thickening fog, and the crowd split left and right, and which to follow? I stood in the gateway and felt my heart hammer.

Something brushed the back of my hand.

I looked down.

I saw a strand of silk, caught on the catch of the gate. A familiar green. Angela's dress.

The strand led away into darkness. Left.

I followed.

50.

A great Army of the Unfortunate and the Insane retreated through the dim streets of north Dublin. The muffled sound of a thousand feet trudging through the heavy fog was intermittently punctuated by wailing, and great shouts of anguish. The Natives were brought to their doors and windows by the wild cries. "Fucking Loopers!" "Bleeding Loonies!" A bottle flew out and down from a balcony, smashing at the shuffling feet of a middle-aged woman. "Care in the Community!" she pleaded up into the fog, in the direction of the high balconies of the tall towers. She had no teeth.

"We are the Community," came a thousand voices, young and old, male and female, from a thousand balconies, through the soft fog.

"Care for us!" cried the Loopers and Loonies, the bad, sad, mad and broken, into the muffled dark, the dark stained yellow and orange by the surviving street lights and the distant burning cars on the fringe of the Estates, where the children were still at play. "We seek Asylum!"

There was a pause.

"Fuck Off," came a thousand voices, and the bottles and cans began raining down.

The Army of the Unfortunate scattered and fled in chaos and terror into the night.

I pursued the silk thread of my love in hints and glimpses, across car-parks and estates, around the shadows of the dead machinery in gaping, broken buildings, through pools of late-night garage light. Her hint flickered through the fog across the empty acres of a deserted market. Over cobblestones.

She sang as she ran.

134

Past a closed Distillery, its machinery polished and exposed now in the roadway, advertising to Americans a bright and empty Public House.

She slapped a hand against the enormous copper still as she swept past. The still rang, a huge and mournful note, low and hollow in the fog as I passed it.

Love's a puzzler.

The unravelling thread had caught again, high on the rivets of the copper cylinder. As I ran after her through the fog, I scooped the drifting, jerking thread into the crook of my right thumb and forefinger, and it slipped through the fork of my hand as I ran.

51.

She sang as she ran. The silk thread ran smoothly through my hand. She turned to the left. I followed. She turned to the right. I followed. Her song had no words, and was beautiful.

She stopped singing.

I reached a crossroads, and the severed end of the thread slid through the V of forefinger and thumb and my hand was empty, held high in the fog.

I stood at the crossroads, and listened, and listened. The sound of the car that had cut the thread faded slowly away into the fog. Silence. Not the sound of a step. No cars, no voices. No one lived in these buildings with no windows. Warehouses? Manufactories? I listened, in all four directions.

A loud crack. Another. Another. A rasping clash.

The crack and clash came to me through the fog, off the flat faces of the low buildings to either side, in double reports, tightly echoed, so that I could not tell their direction. But it was very near: the flat crack and then the loose clash, as though of hurlers both going for a ball and the ash sticks clattering off each other, now flat to flat, now the edges sliding till one catches on the steel hoop binding the wooden face of the other hurl tight. But it was not wood. No. Not two hurleys. Too complex a sound. I looked around, and around. Again the clash.

I looked up.

There they were, two dim figures in the fog. Up on the low flat roof of the building to my left. Near the edge, backing away from each other.

The two men tilted their heads, tilted the huge flat plates of their antlers with their spread of spikes at the edges. Three yards across? Four? I backed across the street to see them better.

The two men ran at each other, the length of the roof, heads tilted till the antlers spread vertically. I blinked as the great antlers clashed, meshed, each set of spikes interlocking with its twin. The men, antlers locked, twisted their heads still further, each trying to gouge the other's flank, or muscle him to the ground. They stood there, swaying, antlers locked, panting a moment. They stepped back, unlocking the spikes of horn, and retreated. Again they came at each other, this time a little too flat, so that they met in a clatter of spikes and bounced apart.

"Excuse me," I said.

They turned their great heads to see me. Each pair of antlers was eight or nine feet across, and added a good three feet to the men's heights.

"Yes?" they said.

"Have you seen a woman pass this way, very beautiful, in a disintegrating dress?"

They turned to look at each other and sighed. They looked back at me and, with difficulty, nodded.

"I thought you were going to ask about the antlers," said the one on the left.

"People normally ask about the antlers," said the one on the right.

"I would be delighted to hear about the antlers, briefly, after you have told me which way she went," I said, not wishing to offend.

"Well," said the left one, "the antlers of the Irish elk..."

"*Megaloceros giganteus.*"

"... have always been subject to furious debate..."

"Were they functional, for combat?"

"Or too delicate for that, and for mere sexual display? Like the tail of the peacock."

"And then it occurred to us, a while back, that there was one good way to find out. The Irish National History Museum has more elk skeletons and elk antlers than any other institution on earth, found perfectly preserved in the rich sedimentary mud of Loch Kiberd. Some are on display, but most of them are stored here, in the Museum's main warehouse. So Todd and I got up on the roof with two fine sets of antlers and tried to move them as the elk would have done... tried to think like the elk... *be* like the elk."

"The most magnificent creatures ever to roam Ireland," said Todd.

"The finest brutes, the biggest beasts..."

"Battling to inseminate a herd of beauties..."

"A dozen doe in heat..."

"Oh yes!" said Todd. "Vivian and I battled on the rooftop, hot, sweating, our antlers clashing above the city."

"With one twist of our heads to the side, like the red stags of Ulster, every tine meshed."

"Every spike locked into place, mine with his, his with mine."

"We had solved the mystery of the Irish elk." They turned to each other, slowly, and smiled.

"But you are still up on the roof," I pointed out.

They swung their great antlers about to look down at me.

"We got to like it," said Todd.

"We discovered better ways to strap them to our heads," said Vivian. "Soon the muscles in our necks developed, to tilt them for combat, to brace for the clash, to wrestle each other to the ground, and roar, and dominate."

Todd let loose a bellowed mating cry across the rooftops, towards the distant Northside towers from whence I'd come.

Vivian continued. "We would leave the antlers on, when going to the pub after work. We were treated with a new respect. No young bucks messed with us, as they had before."

"None mocked our tweeds and eyeglasses."

"If they did, we bellowed in their faces and assumed the battle stance."

"The young bucks turned and left their pints behind, and abandoned the lek, the Battle Place, the rutting ground."

"We drank their pints and took their does."

"All warm and in heat after watching the conflict."

"We are off for a pint now. We drink down by the river."

Todd roared. Far in the distance I heard the little shrieks of excited young women.

"Your woman also went down to the river," said Vivian, pausing, and pointed toward the Quays.

"Thank you," I cried, and turned right, and ran down to the river.

52.

The fog was beginning to lift, as a breeze came upriver from the sea.

I ran down to the Quays, and through the frozen river of vehicles, to the quayside wall. Far below were the broad mudflats of the Liffey, through which a thin trickle of water cut a shallow channel. I looked left and right.

Left.

There. A flicker of green silk, caught on the shattered glass hood of a public telephone.

I ran to it.

The frayed yard of thread was floating, rippling in the thick air, waving, downriver, downriver…

I took a step. The breeze from the sea gave a gust, and the thread toppled over backward in a slow-tumbling wave, and waved upriver, upriver…

I looked left, downriver, right, upriver… I stared at the public telephone.

The plastic piece into which you speak hung, swinging, from its cord. It was shaped like a large bone, as depicted, stylised, in comic books. I bent and lifted it cautiously to my ear, thinking in a confused ecstasy that I would hear her voice, but of course I did not. A thin, high noise, electrical, not human, came steadily out of the top end of the plastic bone. I examined the box of the telephone, with its slots and numbers, and found the place into which the dangling equipment was meant to slot. I put the ball of the bone into its socket, and the thin noise ceased.

With whom had she spoken? Or had a subsequent passer-by let it dangle? I lifted the bone again, and examined it.

There.

On the speaking end, a touch of her lipstick had caught at the edge of one of the little holes. I sniffed it, and thought, perhaps, I could detect a trace of her… Red turned to green in the corner of my vision. The frozen river of cars loosened, liquefied, and flowed downriver, downriver. I closed my eyes and put my lips to where she had put her lips. The plastic was cold. The thin, simple sound in my right ear and the thick, complex roar of traffic in my left ear made me feel weak and empty and I thought I would fall.

Eyes closed, I slipped to my knees on the concrete.

When I opened my eyes, I saw a glint of something, off to my left, downriver, in against the quayside wall. I stood and walked to it.

I bent and took it in my hand.

The tube containing her lipstick.

I uncapped it, and rotated its base, as I had once seen her do. A tiny flat stub of pink scarcely made it to the mouth of the tube. I inhaled its perfume, wound it back into the tube, recapped it.

I put it in the pocket nearest my heart.

I ran.

Downriver.

53.

Trucks roared alongside me. After a while, I found the thread, caught on the rough bark of an old tree. I followed it to the next bridge, where it had been sliced again by traffic. I stood on the corner, and thought.

Left, across traffic and up a broad street.

Right, over a broad bridge.

If she had turned right, over the river, over the bridge, the thread would have continued around the corner, unbroken.

I turned to my left, and crossed the river of vehicles, and walked up the broad street, but could not find the thread. I stopped to ask a passing Nun if she had seen Angela.

"I have seen no girl of that description here," she said.

"And where is here?" I said.

"O'Connell Street, formerly Sackville Street," she said. "The main street of Dublin and therefore Ireland. The aorta of the beating heart of the Nation."

I looked around me.

"And this is the main street of Dublin?" I said, to confirm.

"Yes," she said, smiling. "Dear Dirty Dublin."

A passing child, on his way to the Chip Shop Fight across the street, elbowed his way between us and vomited. Most missed us.

A passing red-faced man in a Nylon Tracksuit halted. "Do ye

want to give us a hand burning out some Blacks?" he said. "Only some of the Lads couldn't make it, and we're making up the numbers."

"No thank you," I replied.

"Fucking poof," said the red-faced man, and spat on my right shoe before moving on.

"Faggot," said a passing girl.

"Fucking faggot," said a passing boy.

"Cunt," said the nun. She blushed. "I'm sorry my son, I have fucking Tourettes."

"Has everyone in Dublin Tourettes?" I enquired.

"No, they are just a bunch of Fucking Cunts," she replied.

"I must confess, I find the atmosphere oppressive," I said, as a small group of Native Dubliners beat an Italian Foreign Exchange Student with a stick and a broken bottle for talking funny.

Blood, piss and vomit flowed in the gutter to swirl away down the storm drain beside us, a Cheese-and-Onion Flavour Tayto Crisp packet rotating gaily on the whirlpool.

"Yes it is currently lacking in that moral uplift proper to our Nation," said the Nun. "But they're doing it up soon. Cunts." She blushed. "Oh, they have great plans for Raising the Tone of O'Connell Street."

"That is good," I said, as a man stabbed a woman for laughing, and two Dublin men kicked the head of a man, just up from the country, whom they had knocked over from behind. "Offaly!" they were shouting. "We'll give you Offaly!"

"You haven't seen my bicycle?" asked the Nun.

"Pardon? No," I said. It was hard to hear her over the noise of the ambulances and trucks and an old man standing weeping beside me. "Where are the Guards?" I said, as a young Dublin man brandishing a bloody syringe took a handbag from a lady tourist.

"Oh, they are up the top end of the street, near Parnell Square, biding their time in case there is trouble later, and keeping an eye on the Asylum Seekers for fear they'd get up to divilment."

I nodded.

A woman on a bicycle, by her dress foreign, hit a deep pothole, and bounced sideways. She disappeared under a truck. Her plastic bag of groceries was thrown from the bicycle carrier, to land right-side-up on the pavement's edge. As the truck's broad rear wheels ran over her head, her brain was popped out of her skull and landed in the gutter almost at my feet. Two citizens of Dublin ran to her side at once, each reaching out to hold a handle of the plastic bag. They tugged in opposite directions a while.

"A right old ding-dong," said the Nun.

The bag at length split and spilled its contents to the road. The two citizens scrambled in the gutter to fill their pockets with the woman's spilled possessions. They fled, leaving only her brain.

It soon floated away on the current of blood and piss and vomit.

"Dear dirty Dublin," said the Nun. "I left my bicycle chained to the front of this pub..." A fire-engine, its windscreen bricked in, tore past. "...But it's gone."

"The bicycle?" I said.

"The pub," she said. "The whole fucking pub is gone."

"Isolde," said the crying man beside me.

"Pardon?" I said.

He blew his nose upon his sleeve. "I *sold* it," he said. "To the Brits. Every stick of furniture. Every beer mat, Guinness ad and ashtray. It's the sixteenth one I've sold them." He turned to the nun. "Your auld bicycle clinched the deal. It's all on the boat to England now. They plan to install it in a pub of excessive Irishness. What do we want with that auld stuff in this New Ireland?"

As he spoke, a young Dublin woman mugged the Nun, who shortly afterwards was taken away in an ambulance.

Workmen arrived, and threw up a sign on the bare fronted building.

A small **b**. An @. An ®. A ©...

142

The old man turned to me. "It is wonderful the way we have transformed Dublin into a modern European capital, retaining the best of the Old, yet gaining the best of the New."

An el. An *on*. An ∀.

There was something strangely familiar about him. And something strangely unfamiliar. I examined him as he coughed up his lunch into his hand, and stood regarding it a while.

Much of it fell swiftly through his fingers.

The solid residue he eventually let fall.

"Hey, where's she gone? Your wan the nun. Her caverns measureless to man." He rubbed his mouth with the back of his hand.

I realised with a shock that this pale, shifty figure was the twitching, wretched shadow of Jimmy "Bungle" O'Bliss. His trousers were stained with a variety of fluids, and you could have boiled his jacket for soup.

"Why Mr. O'Bliss," I said. "Your face is bare."

"I have vomited through my scarf," he said. "A thing not to be recommended. Who the fuck are you?"

And I realised that I had drawn my own rudimentary scarf about my face, to filter the black smoke tumbling from the rear pipes of the buses and the trucks, and that he did not recognise me, his love rival, the man he had once tried to kill. I drew the scarf all the tighter. "My name… is unimportant."

He digested this. "I commend your reserve. You remind me of… myself as a young fellow. And how the fuck do you know me?"

"We have… met," I said.

"And you have sought me out to avenge a wrong, no doubt," he said, squaring up for battle.

"No, our meeting now is the purest coincidence, sir. I came to this city in search of…" I paused. Our love rivalry made this complicated. If I were to name Angela he might recognise me again. And he would not help me find her if he knew. "… Love,"

I finished.

"Love," said Jimmy O'Bliss, relaxing, or collapsing, against the wall. "You're in the wrong city. This is not a City of Love."

"I fear you are right, sir," I said and I was suddenly weary at the admission. I felt a strong urge to lie down on the cold pavement and curl up like a woodlouse into a small ball. Oh, my shoe-heels tight to my buttocks, my knees to my shoulders and my head in my hands...

I looked down in sorrow, and resisted the impulse to lie on the glistening pavement. It had not rained here for a week.

To the sign above us, they added an !

"Paris for Love," said Jimmy O'Bliss, shifting his weight to his left leg, cocking his right slightly. "Galway for... ah, Galway is not the same without the auld swans on the Corrib."

"What happened the swans?"

"I sold them to the Yanks."

Slowly, with great care and concentration evident in his frowning face, he passed a good two pints of air, richly flavoured with the aroma of the famous hops of St. James's Gate, from his anus, while his buttocks encouraged the ongoing achievement with a series of small claps.

When the applause had died down, he continued his speech. "Paris for love. Dublin for the Fumbled Handjob. Dublin for the Drunken Fuck. I was a young man once. I was a young man in Paris. I knew Love!" He roared this last. "I knew Love! The Love you seek, is it an abstract principle or embodied in a particular Woman?"

"Embodied," I replied. "But I have lost her."

"I too, I too, have lost my Love, my Love... I will help you... I will help you find Love. Come, we shall search for your Love." He took my hand. "Join me for a pint and, in the traditional manner of our people, we will drown... drown... drown our sorrows." He pulled me toward **b**@®©e*lon*∀! I made to resist, and resume my quest, but the air filled suddenly with a strange perfume. I felt the fog stir at my back. I heard the door to **b@®©_el_on∀**! open and I swung around in time to catch a glimpse of golden hair and hear a snatch of wordless song. I was afraid of my hope. Jimmy had not seen her. I said nothing but "Yes, I shall join you for a pint."

I swung open the closing door, my mind frantic. Was it Jimmy she had rung? Arranged to meet here, perhaps? No coincidence, then, our meeting... But if that were so, what sly game was he playing now? Had he seen through my disguise? Was he enticing me to my doom?

Passing through the doorway, I saw, caught on a nail-head not yet knocked sufficiently in, the green silken thread.

"Hold up!" said Jimmy O'Bliss, and hauled me back out of the doorway. He was looking up. I looked up.

A man in dusty overalls descended in a cradle from the roof.

"Boss," he said. "There is these huge fucking Bolts in the way, sticking up in the middle of the bowling green."

"Remove them."

"Is that covered by the planning permission?" said the dusty man. He and Jimmy laughed till they wept. There came applause from Jimmy's trousers but it spluttered out. I watched as, after flowing down his inside leg unseen, a steady stream emerged from beneath the turn-up of his trouser, and filled his right shoe with mustard coloured shite.

The dusty man winched himself back up to the roof.

As the flow down Jimmy's inside leg increased, the shoe overflowed till he was standing in a small but rapidly growing pool.

"Quel malheur," said Jimmy O'Bliss.

He hauled me through the door of the pub.

54.

We stepped into the warm, beating, spiritual heart of Ireland: a Dublin pub on a Saturday night.

The green thread still there! Taut, thrumming, the frail thread tangled and snapped before my eyes and was lost in the turbulent human throng. I looked out into a vast space: the smoke rising from a thousand cigarettes softened the view and made it hard to judge distance. Though indoors, we stood on a kind of galleon's deck, edged with bar counters. A little further on, this main deck became an indoor street, lined with large old vehicles leading past a Scottish Presbyterian chapel, toward the silken awnings of a Souk or Bazaar, above which were balconies and further floors, some lit with ultraviolet light, others according to a Japanese theme. Four or five floors above, hanging from the ceiling, was a Viking longship packed with revellers.

"They have the place lovely," said Jimmy O'Bliss.

55.

I scanned the smoking abyss for the woman I loved, but I could not see her.

Jimmy O'Bliss seized my elbow. "I wasn't always a Property Developer, you know. I used to be in Show Business. In the seventies. Wiping archive tape for RTÉ. Of course, it was all wiped by hand in those days, a skilful job. You had your little hand-magnet, and your white cotton glove, and you would spool the tape carefully through your fingers, taking care to hold the magnet flat to the face of the tape..."

My attention wandered for a period of some time as I looked all about, over his head.

"…The first appearance of Peter O'Toole on the Late Late Show, that was one of mine. The first series of Wanderly Wagon… The Rose of Tralee was mine, 1959-1978. And of course all the documentaries, and the drama… By the time I was finished with it, that tape was as good as new. As good. As new. Ah but it was hard, very hard, to just walk away from Show Business…" He steered me to a stool. "What is it you're having yourself? Guinness, is it?"

I nodded, thinking that I would make my escape when he went for the pints. Oh, the cunning of the City!

He moved away to the bar.

I stood and looked about me, helpless. This Pub was larger than any Town in Tipperary. Where to begin? I calmed my rising panic. We were still near the door. She must have passed this way. If she was meeting Jimmy, she'd be hard by. I just had to get to her first. I walked forward slowly, scanning all about me. The deck became a street of cars shaped like rockets, or rockets shaped like cars. I looked closer. The doors had been removed, and the front seats reversed, to make snugs of them.

A man in a suit sat alone in a vast pink car. He caught my eye. I saluted him, and said, "Have you seen the most beautiful woman in the world pass this way, and if so in which direction?"

He stroked his chin. "Why I do believe I have seen the very girl… But allow me to introduce myself. I am Deputy Editor of the Bridge Column of the Irish Times."

"That is a prestigious post," I replied politely, shaking his hand. "In which direction…"

"Indeed it is. All four Deputy Editors of the Bridge Column feel the full weight of that responsibility." He leaned forward, continuing to shake my hand. "I myself have special responsibility for Hearts." He leaned back. "Some would say," he coughed, "that makes me, therefore, senior Deputy Editor. But I like to think of us all as colleagues, as equals."

"It must be onerous, knowing millions read your words in the Newspaper of Record," I said, managing to disengage my hand. I took a step away, in search of information, or the thread, or Angela herself, elsewhere. But he reached out and grasped my elbow.

"Indeed it is. Although, since my promotion from Assistant Deputy Editor of the Bridge Column, First Class, to..." He coughed. "...Deputy Editor, of the Bridge Column, of the Irish Times, with special responsibility for Hearts, I find I have little time myself to write. The administrative responsibilities of the Hearts department fill every waking hour. It is seldom I get to bed before midnight, and I have not seen my children since Michaelmas Eve."

"I can vouch for that," said a uniformed gentleman, standing in the darkness behind the bright vehicle.

"My Driver," said the Deputy Editor of the Bridge Column of the Irish Times with special responsibility for Hearts. "I literally do not know what I would do without him."

"Walk, sir."

"Ha ha ha, very good, Tom, very good." The Deputy Editor's gentle laughter swelled softly to fill the snug, then died away. "The old ones are the best, the old ones are the best... But to return to my theme, there are times when I long to have this burden lifted from me, this crushing weight..."

His grip on my elbow redoubled.

"To be responsible for the careers, the futures, the destinies of a dozen young cubs, a dozen bright and eager First Assistant Bridge Columnists, all hoping one day to make the great leap from the research pool, the sub-editing division, the fact-checkers' gallery, yes, the great leap from the fact-checkers' gallery... to, yes, have some words of their own appear in the Bridge Column of Ireland's Newspaper of Record, in the hallowed pages of the Irish Times itself..."

His breath caught in his throat and he paused a moment.

"Such a burden of hopes, such a weight of others' dreams, can crush a man. Crush... Crush... CRUSH him."

He squeezed my elbow harder with each repetition, and turned his face away for a moment, into the light falling through the open sunroof. The wan beam caught his profile, turning his sparse, silky hair to spun gold. Delicately, I tried to extricate my elbow from his grip. He turned back to face me, and seized my other elbow, almost pulling me into his snug, which rocked on its soft tyres.

"Oh! If you could see their bright, eager faces at the Bridge Column (All–Suits) meetings, in the Great Boardroom of the old Cards & Coarse Fishing Building, abutting the Sport & Ballet Wing of the Irish Times Entertainment and Games Writing Campus...Though of course the Bridge Column is, for historical reasons, considered Cookery..."

My mind wandered, and I scanned, insofar as I could, the crowded space beyond the cars for any hint of Angela. Surely such beauty could not but cause a commotion, a disturbance of the normal that would be visible at a distance?

Nothing.

The drinkers roared, and surged, roared and surged against the bar counters of wood and zinc and marble which jutted out in little jetties, and stood proud in little islands, protected from the force of the surge by a reef of stools.

The Deputy Editor of the Bridge Column of the Irish Times with special responsibility for Hearts squeezed both my elbows hard.

"It rankles!" he said. "Yes, it rankles, when we are accused of being Middle Class. It is nonsense. Why, I myself have a personal friend who has neither Tertiary Degree nor Professional Qualification. Isn't that right, Tom?"

"It is, sir," came the voice from the shadows. "I failed my Inter Cert, Sir," the shadowed figure nodded at me, "on account of the Irish. An N.G. in the Irish. Oh, I rammed the Irish."

"He did. Ah, what with the calumny of those jackanapes at the Irish Independent, the stresses of the job, the burden of responsibility, I confess there are times when I yearn for the day I can retire, my work in this world done. I sometimes fear I am only hanging on for the pension. Oh, let me tell you, there are days when I feel every last one of my twenty-three years. But let me get you a pint. Guinness, is it?"

I nodded, thinking I would pull my old trick and leave when he went to the bar.

"Ah, indeed, your only man, as the fellow said," said the Deputy Editor of the Bridge Column of the Irish Times with special responsibility for Hearts. "Tom, two Guinness and whatever you're having yourself."

Tom emerged from the shadows, nodded to us both, and made his way into the throng surrounding the nearest bar, which was a barge of gold.

I sighed at this setback. My arms grew numb.

"I would go myself," said the deputy editor of the bridge column, "but for this infernal injury," he released my right elbow to stroke his left buttock, following the curve down to the back of the knee. "From last Friday's five-a-side. We thrashed them, thrashed them! It is always a grudge match, the Bridge Column editorial team against the Car Ferry Critics, for historical reasons. Colonel 'Todger' Symons, one of the founding fathers of the Bridge Column and later its senior editor, once damaged one of their gardeners in an off-the-ball scrimmage..."

I shook my right hand, to which blood was returning.

"Of course that was before the abolition of the Hacking rule, when they were still the Sail and Steam Department... How they have come down in the world! They can now barely muster a first eleven for the big tournament at Christmas, and I believe they have no gardening staff at all. Still, that is the modern world for you. Rationalise, cut back... that is all you hear at the Irish Times Annual Strategy Ball..."

I glimpsed the top of Angela's head, entering the Souk or Bazaar, or Harem, and by kicking my interlocutor's left knee and buttock, and gouging his eye with my free hand, persuaded him to let go of my other elbow. I ran through the throng, past the bars, past the cars, and entered the Harem, the Bazaar, the Souk...

56.

I looked about me. A tall man, sprawled on a couch, called across. "Were you seeking that blonde girl who just entered?"

"I was," I said, walking up to him. "I am."

He nodded and drew on his hookah. "These are a marvellous thing. Far easier on the throat than the old briar pipe."

I watched as the smoke gurgled through the water, emerged cooled, ran along the flexible pipe, down his throat and into his lungs. He sighed, "You may kiss my ring."

I kissed his ring.

"What a day," he said. "What a day...! I am just in from the High Court."

"It went well for you, I trust. Did she go...?"

"Victory," said the Bishop. "But at what price..." He reached out and grabbed my hand. "We have won vast damages, against more than thirty-three thousand named children. But the horror, for so many priests and brothers, of having to relive their trauma all over again!" The Bishop choked back a sob. "Some priests were raped thousands of times, by hundreds of children, over a period of decades. It is unlikely they will ever recover. It has destroyed their trust in children. Some, broken, have even taken to drink..."

He shook his head and sighed.

"These poor men, many of them virgins when they entered the priesthood, had their innocence stolen from them by these children. No amount of money can ever restore that innocence. And these children, oh they knew exactly where to go to find their victims. They knew that in the Industrial Schools they would meet the kind of lonely, insecure priest on whom they liked to prey."

He seized my other hand, and squeezed. Water filled his old eyes. And mine.

"A vulnerable man, with no wife or family around him to confide in. And of course the poor priests were afraid to tell anyone. They were afraid they simply wouldn't be believed. Of course nowadays we all know all about Children. I would never leave a priest alone in a room with a Child. But back in those days, you have to understand, the idea that dozens, perhaps even hundreds of Children could rape a priest repeatedly over a period of years never occurred to us. We were very... innocent is the only word for it. It was literally unthinkable. Often a priest would move to another school to escape his tormentors, only to be set upon again."

The bishop sighed. I peered over his shoulder. Was that perhaps a glimpse of...? No.

"But what I think has upset the Hierarchy most is the refusal of the Children to accept responsibility for their actions. Their refusal to come to us and ask forgiveness."

He squeezed. I nodded.

"You are on for a pint, so?" he said, releasing my hands. "To help me celebrate this sorrowful victory?" He rose from the couch, straightened his skirts, and headed for the bar.

I did not wish to stand up a Bishop, but the pursuit of one's true love demands the sacrifice of lesser loyalties. I sprinted through the milling throng, occasionally leaping high, in the hope of glimpsing the top of her head. Among the mingled shouts and cries of the crowd, I briefly thought I heard the roar and clash of bull elk, but the smoke was thick and the bright lights made dark caves of the far corners. The sounds died away with my certainty.

I searched on.

She was not in the Souk, Harem, or Bazaar. I stood at the end of it, on the edge of despair. But one cannot despair. Or rather, one can despair, but it isn't helpful and it doesn't feel pleasant.

I did not despair. I made my way back through the Souk and

stood in the centre of the vast atrium, and looked about me. No sign. I looked around, at the balconies of other floors. No sign. No...

Something tickled the corner of my vision.

Something tickled my ear.

The same thing.

I turned, to see the slimmest thread of green silk shimmer in the smoky scattered light. The point of focus of my gaze ran up and up and up along the green silk thread like the spark along a fuse until it reached...

The longship.

For a wild moment, I contemplated climbing the thread.

No. Better to use the stairs.

More stairs.

A ramp.

I ran.

57.

I reached the longship. She was not there. The thread ended, snapped off, in a crack in a great wooden table, at which sat...

I blinked.

Pat Sheeran.

Reflexively, I put out my hand.

We shook.

"And you are...?" said Pat Sheeran.

Of course, I had had my face rebuilt since he gave me a lift to Galway.

"My name is Ju..." I said, before remembering that I had destroyed his life, and that he wished to kill me. "Is just on the tip of my tongue..."

Yes, 'Jude' had stolen his seat and pissed on the Minister. But he bore no ill will towards the lad to whom he had given the lift… Yet how to explain my new face? It seemed simpler and safer to begin a third identity. But had Barney passed on my message, and defused the problem? Had Barney perhaps even bought the Salmon? How could I ask without revealing my triple identity, as this stranger, and that night-voyager, and also pissing Jude? But I had a more urgent question.

"Your name," prompted Pat Sheeran.

"It will come to me… Have you by chance been sitting opposite the most beautiful woman in the world?" I asked.

"Good God, no," said Pat Sheeran. "On the contrary, I have been sitting opposite…" He paused. "Oh, you must be one of her Galway friends, I'm sorry. Sit." I sat. A happy misunderstanding, whatever it was. "Did I not see you in discussion with the Bishop of Dublin?" He waved overboard, at the Souk far below.

"Perhaps," I said, "for we conversed."

Pat Sheeran frowned once more. "Did he discuss a certain Court Case?"

"He was exulting in victory over the sexually predatory children of Ireland," I said.

Pat Sheeran frowned further. "No mention of a certain pending case which I and others are bringing against him and others?"

"What case would that be, now?" I inquired.

His frowns cleared. "As an absolute convert to the Free Market, to free markets in Wealth, in Goods, in Ideas, I have been led, step by inexorable step, to bring a case involving the Bishop."

"Specify the case," I urged.

"I am suing God for Abuse of Monopoly," he replied. "Our object is to have the Catholic Church in Ireland, as His distributor for the territory, broken up."

"And what inexorable steps led to this outcome?" I asked, buying myself thinking time. For in front of Pat Sheeran was a pint. But across from Pat Sheeran was a glass of Guinness, hardly touched. A woman's drink, the glass astride the table's crack.

Beside it, the broken thread. But no woman…

"The realisation that the Rationalization of Heaven was a disaster," said Pat Sheeran. "The forced consolidation of the innumerable Gods of old Ireland into a single, Three-In-One God, was a catastrophe from which we have not yet recovered. There was a time we had a Spirit in every Blackthorn Bush. You could Negotiate with it. You could get it to mind the house while you were out. And if you fell out with the Spirit in your Bush, and nothing would appease it, well you could move three fields away, and start over with a clean slate. With this Christianity, though, if you fall out with the One God, where do you run to? Where do you hide? No competition, no choice, no alternative. You are ruined. One God, in every field, every tree, every bush. One Effing God. Oh yes, there is the pseudo-competition of the mono-theologies: Judaism versus Christianity versus Islam. But they're nothing but a cartel. They are all the same desert religion, selling the same Abrahamic product. All share the same source-code, which its users are not allowed to modify. And it is the little Gods that suffer: the tree-sprites, the spring-spirits, the fairy in the blackthorn bush. Put out of business. The tree cut down to build a mosque. The spring fenced off as a holy well. The bush burnt under an offering."

I stared at the half pint in front of me, as its head of creamy white went slowly flat and tan. Had Angela sipped from its cold glass lip? If so, would she return? I leaned forward, hoping to see, in the bad light, a trace of her lipstick upon the glass.

"Catholicism was the Operating System installed in all Irish Minds from Independence until recently," said Pat Sheeran. "But it was an abusive monopoly. There was no consumer choice, no competition, and the Irish Government colluded with this disgraceful monopoly by writing the dominance of the Catholic Operating System into DeValera's Constitution of 1936. Thus, I am leading a class action suit against the current Pope, the current Irish Government, and the descendants of Eamonn DeValera."

"Oh," I said. "So you're suing Brünhilde DeValera while also meeting her about the Salmon of…" I bit my tongue.

Pat Sheeran gave me a look. "So you know about the Salmon…" He scratched the back of his neck. "In fact, my meeting with Brünhilde DeValera over the Salmon of Knowledge was a ruse. My true intention was to serve her with legal papers in front of witnesses." He gave me another look. "Perhaps I know you from the Movies?" He frowned. "Your face is familiar…"

"I am told I resemble the actor Leonardo DiCaprio," I said.

"Ah, that must be it." He ceased to frown, and I relaxed.

"And is there something wrong with the Catholic Operating System?" I enquired, trying to change the subject, while staring at the little glass, my face lowered. Yes, I thought, there is a trace… I kissed the pink.

Pat grew animated. "Faults in the Catholic Operating System were acknowledged as early as the publication of the recommendations of Vatican II! But that was already too late for me! I'd missed the Sixties!" He calmed. "Our case is strong. Indeed, recent precedents in the US against the Corporate Capitalist Bill Gates and his Windows Disc Operating System Monopoly have hugely strengthened our case. The Church are very vulnerable, too, on the issues of consent, cooling-off periods, refunds, return of goods and termination of contract. Also complaints procedures. No other product is forced upon screaming children who are in no position to give informed consent at the time of installation. Oh, the tobacco companies have nothing on these fellas. And you can't leave! There's no escape clause in the contract! I've been trying to get excommunicated for years, but they just bounce you around from department to department. If a credit card were issued on such terms the bank would lose its license… But you look as though you have a Question," he said.

I nodded. "What is an Operating System?" I said.

"An Operating System, or religion, is essentially a set of rules for processing the information the world throws at us. It is designed to give the system stability. Once you have the rules installed, you can communicate with others running the same set of rules, and even join together in faith-based networks or communities. Trying to communicate with anyone using a different set of rules may lead to incomprehension and conflict. In all key respects, Catholicism is an Operating System. It is installed in us at baptism, and upgraded on a regular basis, by qualified technicians, first at holy communion, confirmation..."

I was saved from further explanation by the arrival of a stranger at our table. My heart rose.

My heart fell. A man. In a suit.

He coughed.

"I could not help but hear you speak disparagingly of Catholicism, Christianity and indeed the three major branches of Monotheism, and compare them unfavourably to Free Market Capitalism."

"You heard me right," said Pat Sheeran.

The man nodded. "I believe this is a false opposition, for they operate in different realms. Indeed, Free Market Capitalism could not exist without Christianity: it is Christianity's bastard child. As Max Weber argued, in 'The Protestant Ethic and the Spirit of Capitalism', the early Protestants saw economic success as a sign from God that one was of the Heavenly Elect. It reassured one that one was saved. Well, it was a simple step from that to *prioritising* economic success, as a way of *ensuring* one would be saved. Thus, as Walter Benjamin so brilliantly argued in 'Capitalism as a Religion', Capitalism silently took over Reformation Christianity and replaced the religion with itself. It became a religion: *the* western religion. Thus when Protestantism arrived in America in its purest form, so did Capitalism. Thus the Catholic Spanish Americas never throve economically, in contrast to the Protestant, Anglo-Saxon North Americas. Thus the collapse of Catholicism in Ireland over the past decade exactly mirrors the rise of Capitalism in Ireland. The Celtic Tiger is Protestant."

We mused on this. He took a sip of his pint and continued, as several nearby drinkers shuffled closer, along the long table, the better to follow the argument. "We have undergone a Reformation, with Mary Harney of the Progressive Democratic Party as Martin Luther. But it is possible to have the best of both worlds, and I believe I do. For I myself am both Believer and Entrepreneur."

The nearby drinkers shuffled closer still.

"And how do you combine the Oil of Belief, and the Water of Entrepreneurship?" said Pat Sheeran.

"I franchise the fingers of Saint Malachi."

"Is that a fact?"

The man nodded and held out his hand. "Myles Christie," he said. We all shook. "For as little as ten grand down, I give you both a Territory, and a Finger. Of course, a lot of hard work goes into building up a franchise. Relics were traditionally marketed in an ad hoc way, seldom maximising the value of the franchise. For every head of Saint Andrew in St. Peter's…"

There was a general nodding from the nearby drinkers. "I touched it myself," said a short, hairy man. "It had cured my wart within the year."

"…there was a heart of St. Valentine."

There was a meditative silence. "God, I'd forgotten Saint Valentine," said a tall bespectacled woman at length.

"Exactly! The Patron Saint of Lovers! Beaten to death with clubs and had his head cut off! A magnificent brand gone to wrack & ruin through mishandling. His *entire corpse* was given as a gift to the people of Ireland, in 1836, by Pope Gregory XVI. The entire Saint was brought in Solemn Procession to Our Lady of Mount Carmel church in Whitefriar Street. Then what did they do? With the corpse of Saint Valentine, no less? A world class treasure trove of relics, with an incalculable breakup value?"

"What?" said various drinkers, leaning forward.

"They put him into storage! In a cardboard box! Saint

Valentine! I only tracked him down last year, and immediately bought out the Carmelites. Storage!" sighed Myles Christie. "Oh, we could learn a lot from the Buddhists. The Buddha's tooth, in The Temple of the Tooth, in Kandy, Sri Lanka, for instance. Great presentation. Solid gold container. And the endless stream of tourists! Five thousand years of 'offerings'! It puts us in the ha'penny place. And by Jesus, the new lads aren't too slow off the mark either. Medina! And Mecca! That meteorite in the Kaaba, by God! A white rock, dyed black by blood-offerings. Not an obvious hit. Purely local, pagan, in a backwater. But the Islamic lads, fair play to them, built it up into a global brand, re-launched it, put in the tourist infrastructure, and it's pulling in two million tourists a year. Re-brands work. And Saint Valentine is a dream candidate for a total re-brand. Thanks to Valentine's Day, there is crossover potential, not only into the general Christian market, but also the rapidly expanding New Age and post-Christian markets. And we can multiply our marketing spend and impact by coordinating with the greeting card, flower and chocolate industries. That is the Future. We bought up some of the Abolished Saints recently too. Prices dropped after the official confirmation that they didn't exist, but they're still strong, strong brands. Oh, existence is a *bonus*, sure, but people put too much store by it. We picked up some fantastic bargains in the panic. I'll be launching the leg of Saint Juliana of Nicomedia in Medjugorje at Christmas. And I'm taking St. Christopher's spleen on tour in the Spring."

"Oh, where to?" asked a young man in a T-shirt bearing the slogan

FATIMA MANSIONS

KEEP MUSIC EVIL

in bright red letters. "The mother is a huge fan of St. Christopher."

"The States, Mexico, Brazil, and we're doing one night only in Dusseldorf," said Myles Christie. "The jetlag will be sickening, but the money was right." "Oh the mother could make Dusseldorf. Sure, Ryanair fly to Dusseldorf."

There was a brief diversion, as the short hairy man argued with the tall bespectacled woman over whether Saint Juliana of Nicomedia had been burnt, boiled, beheaded, or crucified. This diverted the conversation onto the subject of crucifixion generally, and the argument grew heated. Myles Christie was brought in as arbitrator, being an expert in religious mutilation.

"I have often found fault with the nail-placement in statues of the crucified Jesus Christ," said Myles Christie. "Frequently nails are driven through the flesh of the palms, an absurd and senti-mental convention."

"But," said the short hairy man, "It delivers the visual excitement of fingers splayed in agony, rather than the visually bland limp hands of a wrist piercing."

"But at what cost to realism?" said Myles Christie. "The weight of the body can not, in fact, be supported thus without the nails tearing through the thin palms and the delicate webs between fingers."

The bespectacled woman nodded, murmuring "My point exactly. Which of course leaves the body, nailed at the feet, to topple forward…"

Myles took over, "…either breaking the ankles, tearing free of the final nail, or rotating about the final nail to hang upside down by the feet. The weight of the body then rips the nail through the flesh of the lower foot, and out. Can't be done."

"But," said the hairy man, "surely the palm piercings are largely decorative, it's the legs support the weight? Your man stands on a slanted step or wedge. Even the foot-piercing is semi-decorative, designed chiefly to prevent the feet slipping off the slanted step."

I sat back and enjoyed the vigorous debate. It reminded me of similar arguments, raging for days, every Easter at the Orphanage. The larger Lads eventually nailed up a small Orphan, in the Orchard, to demonstrate their theories. His howls alerted Brother Ryan who released him with a crowbar, and demonstrated the orthodox and approved method on those he deemed to be the three ringleaders. Tom Kinsella objected strongly to not being crucified higher and more centrally than Noel Kenny and Waxy Tracey. In the end, Brother Ryan relented, partially. "You can be the thief who was Saved," he said, and re-nailed Tom up a foot higher, which mollified him somewhat.

I returned mentally to the conversation.

"...but Fingers are my first love," Myles Christie was saying. "My dream is to find the Finger that Saint Thomas poked into the hole in Jesus..." He sighed, and shook his head. "Ah, a man can dream... But yes, as relics, Fingers have unlimited potential."

"But did God not give man a limited number of fingers?" asked the short hairy man.

"He did indeed, and it is precisely that limitation which has always held back the finger-franchising industry," said Myles Christie, nodding. "What is the point going to all the effort and expense of building up a brand if you can only create ten franchises? The toe market gives you a little room for expansion, but not much. Toes are never as big a draw as fingers, and never will be. I keep out of the toe business entirely. Of course, the promotion of *generic* Saints' Fingers was always an option."

"Ah," said the short hairy man. The tall bespectacled woman frowned, and opened her mouth.

"Oh, I know," said Myles Christie. "In as much as it expanded the overall market for relics it was a good thing, but half the time you were only robbing Peter to pay Paul, literally mind you. And you could never get all the Saints' representatives to agree on an overall strategy, or to contribute their fair share to the marketing budget. There is always one cute hoor," said Myles Christie abruptly, "naming no names, a certain Saint pierced by

161

arrows… we'll say no more… a certain gay icon who shall remain nameless…"

A vein was throbbing energetically in his right temple and his right eyelid began to twitch.

"…whose people were quite happy to sit back and reap the benefits of a collective campaign into which they had not put one brass farthing…That fucker Saint Sebastian, if you'd be listening to them fellas, had more arrows put into him than… than… arrows! What kind of a relic do you call arrows, then, hah? A fancy name for a stick. And them charging fifty thousand smackeroos the franchise! And getting it! For a stick! And a territory not big enough to wipe your arse on! It's them buckos bring the whole game into disrepute."

He brooded briefly.

"But you have overcome the limits God imposed upon the exploitation of Saint Malachi's fingers," said Pat Sheeran helpfully after a time.

"I have." The lines upon the forehead of Myles Christie vanished. "I have. You see, it is all about building trust, all along the supply chain. Authenticity is what the customer craves. But they have to trust you. It has to be authentic, and it has to be *scientifically proven* to be authentic." He lowered his voice. "And we've cracked it."

All shuffled closer, the better to hear.

"We buy fingers from the poor, often after industrial accidents. If fingers cannot be medically reattached, they are of no use to the hospital, or their former owners. To ensure security of supply, we have informal agreements with several NHS hospitals in the UK, and many Accident and Emergency units in the developing world. China is an increasing source of Fingers. Your Chinese finger is a fine finger, delicate, almost spiritual. Ideal for my Device."

"You have a Device?" said Pat Sheeran, leaning closer.

"I have," said Myles Christie, leaning back. "You attach your severed finger to my Device. It flushes the semi-congealed blood from the veins and capillaries, giving the required, pale, spiritual appearance to the finger. It then circulates a neutral fluid loaded with a tailored virus which is, in turn, loaded with DNA cloned from the single surviving authorised finger of St. Malachi."

All gasped.

"The virus targets the dermal and sub-dermal cells of the new finger, and delivers the authentic DNA of St. Malachi to *each and every one*. This authorised copy is then *indistinguishable* on a casual DNA test from that of St. Malachi himself."

All gasped.

"Well..." He frowned. "There is still also an awful lot of the DNA of the original Chinese woman present, but we are working on that. This will do for relics what photography did for oil painting!"

Some gasped. Some scratched their heads.

"And we aim to be the Eastman Kodak of that revolution."

All applauded. Some subscribed for shares in his Initial Public Offering.

I sensed someone arriving behind me. The sense in question was that of smell.

"There you are," said Jimmy O'Bliss. The crowd moved a little away from him, as he cracked my pint down on the table. The long table shook. The longship shook. A little dust fell from the dark rafters above, from which the steel cables descended.

"Sir," said Tom, shimmering into view at my elbow. He put down my pint beside Jimmy's black gift.

"My dear boy!" said the Bishop of Dublin, "Here you are!" He slapped down my pint by the other two, the meat of his hand and the glass bottom thumping the table. Table and longboat shook.

They continued to shake.

More dust fell from above.

A large, rusty, metal nut fell into the first of my pints. We all looked up, along the cables holding the longship aloft, into the rafters. Something squeaked.

Something moved.

Another nut fell, striking the long table and bouncing off it, overboard, and down into the distant crowd.

Far below, people began to scream, and move away from under us. All except two familiar figures, locked in combat on the dance floor, unable to retreat, unable to advance...

One of the cables lost tension. The boat lurched, and the cable came coiling down at us and we all stepped back with a gasp, or sigh, as it fell in steel loops across the table, spilling and smashing my three pints.

I stared at Jimmy and Jimmy stared at me.

"The bolts on the roof..." he started.

"Hold up this ship..." I finished.

A nut fell past.

Another.

Two more cables gave way. The ship lurched down. The railed gangway out to the ship bent and groaned.

Walking across it toward me, in a band of green silk and no more, was...

The gangway snapped off behind her, as another cable gave. The force of the gangway explosively straightening beneath her feet threw her forward, so that she landed, somewhat untidily, aboard the ship.

The last two cables snapped, or the bolts gave, or the old wood, and we were falling through the smoky air in a Viking longship and all the drinks and ashtrays were shifting and sliding gently down the tilting table as we held on to it, to the benches, to the sides...

The plunge to our doom was unusually slow.

The impact was curiously cushioned.

I lifted myself from the floor of the ship, and looked over the side. Panels of veneer had popped off the outside as we landed, to reveal thick slabs of polystyrene. They had compressed and cracked and absorbed the energy of our fall.

Sticking out from under the ship were two sets of vast antlers.

Jimmy O'Bliss staggered to my side. "You have killed them surely," he said. "The only Elk Paleontologists of the Western World."

But I was looking past him, at Angela. She stood, and leaped over the shattered side of the ship, into the returning crowd.

I followed.

Jimmy followed.

We stood in a triangle, for it is almost impossible for three people to do otherwise and still talk. The crowd cleared a space for us.

"Oh Angela," I said.

"Ya slut," said Jimmy O'Bliss.

"I love you," I said.

"I love you," said Jimmy O'Bliss. Then he looked at me. I realised my face was not covered.

Jimmy stared at my unscarfed face. I stared at his. Angela silently stared at both of us, then slipped away into the crowd.

"You!" said Jimmy O'Bliss. "Back to avenge the honour of your woman, eh? I should have finished you the first time." And he came for me.

I wrenched a set of antlers from Vivian's head, to protect myself from Jimmy's assault.

Jimmy seized the other set from the unconscious Todd.

The antlers were heavy and unwieldy. I held him off with mine, as he stabbed at me with his. My arms grew tired, wielding their broad shields. I lifted them, and slipped my head into the helmet and straps.

Jimmy, breathing hard, did likewise.

The antlers sat snug, and I swung my head from side to side.

The floor cleared. Strength ran through me and I was no longer tired. Jimmy roared, and ran at me.

We clashed, rattled, bounced off each other. I tilted my head, on a reflex, and Jimmy did the same, and ran at me again.

We locked, hard. Braced, feet wide, we twisted our heads, roaring, the locked antlers swaying, twisting, and I gave a great lurch, with the muscles of my shoulders roaring in pain, and my long tines pierced Jimmy's flank and with another lurch I had him gutted and his life-blood and shite and black porter leaked slowly from his old bowel across the floor.

I tore another strip from my coat lining and covered his pale face with the improvised scarf.

The old men gasped in recognition. "'Tis Jimmy O'Bliss..." All removed their hats.

The old men gathered over Jimmy's antlered corpse.

"That man had a book in him."

"Oh such a book as he had in him."

"The like of which you'd not see today."

"By Jesus, no. My God that man had a book and a half in him."

"He did."

"He did."

"He did."

A nearby barman paused briefly in his pouring. "He did."

"It was going to be a novel that tore the lid off things, by Jesus. That tore the lid off."

They pondered this. Another spoke up. "No. No, it was going to be a history of Dublin that would put all your fellows in Cambridge on their ear. On their ear."

"Oh, back in their box all right. And the Oxford lads with them."

All nodded and sighed.

"And oh, he was a great debater."

"The greatest. The greatest."

"The time he called Maudy Cooney, and in the finest tones, and himself standing on a chair, he just stands up on the chair, not a note or anything, it just came naturally to him, he had the gift, and he calls, in ringing tones, a hush, a hush fell at the sight of him, he was so formidable a foe in debate, and he calls Maudy Cooney an auld cunt! Just like that. Didn't even have to think about it. 'Point of order, Mr. Chairman, Maudy Cooney is only an auld cunt!' Quick as that. It came to him as easy as breathing."

"Oh, you should have heard him."

"A character."

"A character."

"A real auld Dublin character."

"A real Dub."

"A Dub."

"...Dub," mumbled a nearby snoozing boozer briefly from his barstool, before snoring once more.

Once I had recovered my wind, I looked about me. I did not see Angela. I did not see Pat Sheeran.

"It is fitting that Jimmy O'Bliss should die on this very spot," said the Deputy Editor of the Bridge Column of the Irish Times with special responsibility for Hearts.

"My God, yes."

"The very spot on which he spewed upon the Brogues of William Smyllie," said the Deputy Editor.

The old men put on their hats again, in order to take them off.

"They Laminated the Vomit," said Pat Sheeran, returning. He pointed to a large plaque, bearing a mounted object, high on the far wall, indistinct in the gloom. "It was the only relic of the old place that Jimmy wouldn't sell."

"Where is she?" I said.

Pat looked up from the corpse. "Who?"

"The woman you were drinking with. Angela."

"Oh. Her. She's just borrowed a grand off me, and she's on her way to catch the ferry to a job in London. Whatever job she's lined up requires an awful lot of new underwear."

I ran.

A stitch afflicted me. I slowed, temporarily, to a walk.

The thread had caught on the same nail, on her way out the door.

58.

I emerged into silence.

I looked about me.

The guards had blocked off O'Connell Street for a hundred yards either side of the General Post Office, and cleared the area. I went up to a guard.

"Is it on account of my slaying of Jimmy O'Bliss?" I inquired, the gore dripping from the tines of my antlers.

"Eh? No. We're about to Raise the Tone of O'Connell Street. Feck off like a good fellow, and don't be bothering me."

I shrugged, and caught the silken thread, and walked straight across the broad deserted Street, to a shop whose windows displayed impractical clothing. The thread was caught, high, at the joining of closed doors of pink glass. I stood before the doors. They opened silently. As they parted, the unbroken thread fell softly to the floor.

I stepped inside and I looked around. All about me stood mannequins displaying further impractical clothing.

A smiling woman greeted me. "Are you looking for anything in particular, sir?" she said. "Anything... special?"

"Yes," I said.

"And what would that be, sir?"

"Love," I said humbly.

"Wise Guy," she said, and turned away.

Blushing at the compliment, I followed the thread in among the mannequins and down stairs, toward a sound resembling the murmuring of innumerable bees.

59.

At the bottom of the stairs I stood, transfixed.

All about me were women in couples and groups, giggling and laughing. The air was intricate with their mingled perfumes. In their hands many held penises of plastic and rubber, some vibrating.

The silken thread led through the crowd, under breasts quivering with laughter, past navels filled with jewels and steel, straight to the ragged hem of my first love's green dress. The thread, in its repeated journeys back and forth, around the circumference of the dress to the seam and back, to the seam and back, to the seam and back, had unravelled the dress from ankle to armpit. All that was left of it ran in a single thin band of silk about her collarbones, beneath her arms, around her back, held from falling by her bare breasts.

She stood there in her perfection.

Now, I would declare my love. Now, I would ask her to grow old with me. I had acquired the face she had demanded. I would accumulate the wealth, out in the broad world. All I wished to tell her was that my love was true, and strong. All I wished to ask her was to wait for me, for I would not be long.

I stepped forward, into her perfume.

Oh my love!

Perhaps I should tell her, too, that I had just slain her lover. I knew from observing the Love Affairs of the Lads back in the Orphanage that it is often these little things, which seem so inconsequential that we do not think to mention them, which rankle with a girl if she should find them out later from a third party.

I paused, to think. Yes I should definitely tell her.

Oh, that fatal pause!

As I stepped forward, the glass doors and windows of the floor above were kicked in by the massed ranks of Dublin's Gardaí.

Women shrieked and hid, as the officer corps pounded down the steps, gasping, followed by their men.

"Oh Ho! Oh Ho!" they shouted, "Here, on this ground, this day, Catholic Ireland makes its last stand! How're ye, Ladies! This shop, Ann Summers Foreign English Knicker and Vibrator Shop, with an address at 30 to 31 O'Connell Street, Dublin, is hereby busted, for Lowering the Tone of O'Connell Street."

"Ladies," said their Chief, shaking his head, "was it for this that the heroes of 1916 died, across the road in the GPO? So the barefoot maidens of Ireland," he indicated Angela, "could pleasure themselves with English machinery, while wearing English knickers? Was it for *this* that Wolfe Tone died?"

A tremulous chorus of guards, bunched above him on the stair, sang a sweet bar of Amhrán na bhFiann, and we all stood to attention and joined in. When they reached verse three, celebrating the slaughter of the Saxon Foe, my heart swelled with fierce pride and I sang all the louder. A reflex from my hurling days, as a back on the Orphanage under-12 team. If time was short before a match, we would often start with verse three for fear of missing it.

The Ladies wept. "Oh dear God, forgive us!" they cried. Angela, I noticed, had edged away toward a silver pole, or pillar, and was surreptitiously selecting knickers.

"Was it for this DeValera died chastely in his bed?" went on the senior Guard in a softer tone. "So that ye could purchase… plastic… Pleasure?"

"No, no, stop!" they sobbed.

"Go back to your husbands, Ladies," whispered the Guard. "Go back to your husbands, and do your duty."

"We will! We will, Guard!" they wept, and the Garda Choir on the stairs, still singing softly, parted to let the women pass, heads bowed, in single file.

I looked back at Angela, her right hand full of knickers, her left of bras. Yes, the second the National Anthem ended, I would run

170

to her and declare my love. But as I watched, she pulled herself, hand over hand, up the silver pole, her bare feet providing grip. Vaulting lithely over the balcony rail, leaping from the shoulders of startled Guard to startled Guard to avoid the glass–strewn floor, she made her way out through the empty windows and into the street, into the night, into the world…

Had ever a man been torn so, between love of Woman and of Nation? I and all the guards stood to attention as the Garda Choir added high harmonies to the last, stirring verse.

The final yards of silken thread fell softly, in swirls and loops, down from the balcony, to drape us weightlessly.

And how would I ever find her now?

The last of the women left. The National Anthem ended. The guards filled their pockets with evidence, and smashed up the shop. I made my way up steps sparkling with shattered glass and women's tears, to the street. I removed the heavy helmet of my antlers and dropped them to the sparkling ground.

On the empty pavement in the empty street I howled at the sky a while.

Then I remembered. The ferry to London.

I ran…

60.

I got to the pier's end just as the largest car ferry in the world was pulling out.

"Shite," I said.

A small sailboat pulled up at the pier, below me.

I called down to the couple sailing her. "Excuse me, but would you help me catch up with that ferry?"

The man standing on deck snorted. "Certainly…" he said, "…not. My God, you don't want to follow *that* ferry."

His female companion nodded.

"She lacks gravitas," he said. "Worse, the name of that car ferry carries no mythic import."

"Should it?" I said.

"If I built a car ferry," said the man, his voice rising greatly in pitch, perhaps with passion, "the name of my car ferry would carry Mythic Import."

"Too many rivets," said the woman, climbing the ladder up to the pier.

"*Riveting*," said the man, following her up, his head bobbing in and out of view from behind her buttocks, "is all very well if you are into that sort of thing. *I* am not."

"Far too much forward momentum."

"Too much *thrust*."

"Why, she is not a proper Irish car ferry at all," said the woman, arriving up beside me, "For she spends half her time in British Waters."

"Pandering to the British Market," said the man, arriving up after her. "Oh, dear dirty Dublin isn't good enough for her. I happen to have here the plans for my own, unfinished, car ferry." He handed them to me.

"Ah," I said, studying them.

"My car ferry," he said, looking back out to sea, his eyes unfocusing, "will display a great deal of gravitas and bear a name which will carry more Mythic Import than that of any car ferry currently in service."

"His will be a truly Irish car ferry," added the woman, "aimed at Irish people, travelling the Dublin to Dublin route solely, and without leaving Irish territorial waters. I see her as being in the tradition of the great 20th century German car ferries of the Rhine and the Ruhr."

"You are not by any chance Car Ferry Critics for the Irish Times?" I said.

"We certainly are!" said the man.

"Indeed, *I…*" the woman gave a little cough, "…am Chief Car Ferry Critic for the Irish Times."

"And you will not help me out into the World?"

"And leave dear dirty Dublin?"

"We will not do you that disservice."

I thanked them, and stole a canoe.

Paddling my own canoe, I left behind the Dubliners, and drew alongside the largest car ferry in the world, taking care not to be overwhelmed by the Wake.

61.

I climbed the proud rivets of her pale flank, and swung aboard.

I searched the ship for Angela, as Ireland shrank behind me, and was gone.

Finally I found her, at the very prow of the vast vessel. For warmth, she wore all her new panties, bras, and other, more complex forms of underwear, leaving only her midriff, upper thighs, neck, lower back and a small number of other curves of flesh exposed to the cold air and the fog.

"Angela," I said.

My nose shrank in the curiously cold air, and I could feel myself become again the Living Spit of Leonardo DiCaprio.

Angela circled me slightly, and drew back one foot.

I backed into the V of the handrails at the very nose of the ship, which she had just left. I felt boneless and weak. But the little strength remaining to me entered my voice.

"I love you," I said.

My words seemed somehow to melt her reserve. There was a general softening of her surfaces, though perhaps this was just the thickening fog. She unfolded her arms, ceased to frown, and returned to the deck of the ship the foot which she had previously pulled back in preparation, if necessary, to kick me.

My heart leapt at this sign of affection. This was the great moment toward which I had been traveling, entirely unaware it loomed so vast in my future, for all of my life. I surveyed her beauty and savoured the rich flavour of this Moment of Moments.

Perhaps distracted by something over my right shoulder, she turned her cheek toward me a trifle. This, this was it... my invitation... my opportunity... my destiny...

She grasped the rails to either side of her, hard, with both hands, as if to brace herself for the inevitable.

I leaned my warm lips toward her pale cheek.

62.

It was unfortunate that, at that very moment, having travelled halfway round the Irish coast on the north-westerly currents of the Atlantic's Gulf Stream, and the south-westerly currents of the bleak North Sea, Charles J. Haughey's private iceberg loomed suddenly up out of the fog and tore open the world's largest car ferry the full length of her Hull, down her left flank, some metres below the waterline, causing her to sink.

The smooth course of our true love was disrupted by the impact, for the collision threw me backwards over the guardrail.

I hurtled, rotating, toward the iceberg.

"Wait for me my love, I shall swiftly retu..." I cried, before hitting the glistening side of the berg with an unmerciful blast of déjà vu...

63.

When I came to, my bruised face throbbing, it was to see Charles J. Haughey looming over me. His gut had gone. His shoulders had broadened. The hank of hair which traditionally crossed the smooth dome of his head from right to left, now hung down, obscuring the right-hand side of his face. Above his single, shining eye, the hoarfrost glittered thick upon lash and brow. The full moon was clearly visible, high overhead, through the thin, sea-hugging layer of fog. In his right hand he clutched what appeared to be a human thighbone. Between his own parted thighs I could see the enormous bulk of the ferry, standing on her stern about a mile beyond him. The moon's fog-smudged light illuminated the dim white form of the dying ship. Two thirds submerged, she lurched lower in the water even as I watched.

"You," said Charles J. Haughey. "Little. Fucker."

64.

Through the thinning fog, I saw a wriggling speck atop the tip of the drowning ship. Angela, or a bent lash in my own eye? I blinked, winked, and blinked again.

"Oh, flutter those pretty lashes all you like. Your coquettish tricks will avail you naught, out here where Men are Men." Charles Haughey hauled back his right arm. Seams popped and split: seams of lining and of cloth. He took a deep breath, and roared. Another seam popped. He drew back further his right arm.

I looked up at him, startled.

The ball-joint of the hip-bone he wielded eclipsed for an instant the small, full moon. The accelerating mass of the swung bone toppled him backwards, his smooth heels rotating on the wet ice. Winded, he lay still on the ground.

The iceberg, too, was rotating. It turned clockwise on the face of the ocean, having found some new current, or been found.

Behind Charles Haughey's bulk of shredded suit cloth, the full panorama of the rescue swung slowly into sight. The giant ship was surrounded at a little distance, to avoid the suck of her going down, by rescue boats: two trawlers, some sailboats, a cargo ship. A bright orange lifeboat. Half a dozen of its own little white lifeboats. For how long had I been unconscious? Were they rescuing the last, or the first, of the passengers? Did my warm love live yet, or was she cold in the cold water?

The distant rescuers swung slowly out of sight, behind a wall of ice. Soon, all were gone. The rotating sea was empty of ships, and light, and land.

65.

I struggled to my feet on the difficult surface, and made to help Charles Haughey to his.

"Fuck off," he said, swinging the hip-bone up at me.

I took back my hand, and turned, and walked away.

She had been rescued, or she had died, as I lay numb and unconscious on the cold ice. Other hands had held her, had plucked her from the deck. Or they had not... I did not wish to think of this.

I explored the dim rotating island, as I grew increasingly numb.

She lived.

She died.

She lived.

The surface was treacherous and the ever-changing angle of the circling moonlight made distances misleading. After my second fall, I decided to leave further exploration till the morning. I slept in my clothes in a gully.

Deep in the night, I jerked awake from a dream with a shock and a spurt of adrenalin. I thought I saw her shimmer, a nude figure in the fog and ice and moonlight. I thought I saw her wave and smile and whisper as the waves whispered far below against the ice. Jude... Oh, Jude...

I blinked. There was nothing but a curve of ice in moonlight. But I knew, nonetheless, that it was true.

She lived.

She lived.

She lived.

There was nothing I could do, for now. "Be patient," I told myself. I mused on the Latin root. *Pati*. Suffer.

Eventually, when the adrenalin had soured and faded, I fell back to sleep. There were no more dreams.

Pink through my lids, the dawn light woke me. I set out to explore the floating crystalline island.

66.

There was little to explore. The once massive ice-island was sadly diminished. Much of the bridge of the nose had collapsed, the cheeks had sunk, the brow had lowered, and the hairline had receded. All was sun-pocked, shrunken, gullied by melt-water. Charles Haughey had chipped small steps up to the great nostrils but decay had deepened and enlarged the steps, merging two, then three together. I made my way up in great strides, till I stood at the thinned septum, a vast dark cave to either side. The two great nostrils had hollowed out still further, great caverns now in the ice.

I entered the vast right nostril, and I saw, deep in the blue gloom, a flicker of movement.

I walked deeper into the hazy blue light, one hand out ahead of me, for distance was again a treacherous thing in this translucent, uneven, half-melted space. When I had reached the thing that flickered, I crouched.

White, tinted blue by the light and ice, it was next to invisible. The ribcage of Dan Bunne, clean of all flesh. Inside the cage was a large black bird. As it walked back and forth, its black feathers were eclipsed and revealed in alternating stripes by the white bones, so that it seemed to flicker.

As my eyes grew accustomed to the gloom, I saw the grey feathers on the neck and body. Black wings. Black head.

A scald crow.

I heard the creak of tired ice behind me, and turned. Haughey stood framed in the archway of the nostril.

"Beautiful, isn't she?" he said, and walked to my side. "I am sorry I tried to kill you. A spasm of my old Self." The scald crow stared at us, and we at her. "You brought me to this new life: I should thank you."

The crow shrugged her wings, and spread them, closed them. She shuffled her feet, and, without looking away from us, stepped up onto a loose human vertebra lying detached on the ice. I noticed the heads and dark guts of smaller birds, lying in pink patches on the ice floor of the cage. The scald crow looked away from us, and lunged at a tern's detached head. She pierced its eyeball, and then methodically worried the deflated sac loose. Severing the optic nerve with a sawing tug, she threw back her head to swallow the soft orb.

"Ah, natural nature at her most natural," said Charles Haughey. "It is better than the Television."

Later, we sat in the cave mouth talking.

"I am curiously happy," said Charles J. Haughey. "The Bird here, I have taught the calls of other Birds. Her cries lure them to this cave, and I sweep them from the air with Dan's old bones.

Gulls, terns, guillemots... All my old hurling skills have come back to me. It is as though I had just pulled on the gansey for the first time: the years melt away, and I squint into the blue sky, as though seeking a high, wild ball descending from a distant clash of the ash in midfield, falling from out of the sun. And the old crow calls behind me, and in swoops a black-headed tern, into the darkness, and I swing in that instant when he is still blind, and he is plucked from the air and flung to the cold ice. And in that instant I am mighty Finn, I am Cúchulain, I am as a God..." He closed his eyes, and swung an imaginary bone, or hurley. The final seam split, up the back of the jacket, and it fell apart, in two halves, each sliding down the silk of his shirted arm and falling to the dim ice.

He opened his eyes and sighed, in his shirtsleeves.

"For a while I shot birds from the sky but I am down now to my last shell. And, once, early on, I shot an albatross. That, I regret. The albatross, high, solitary, circling the world, so far above the petty squabbles of the lesser birds..."

We sat in companionable silence.

All I could hear was the splash of the waves, and the creak of the ice.

67.

Two days later, we sighted land. To the East: Britain's shore.

Hot desire rose in me till I trembled and was almost sick. Angela walked that land, or soon would. No, a shipwreck would not stop her. I would find her in London.

I prepared to leave. I slipped the scrap of paper containing the clue to the secret of my origins into my True Love's lipstick. I put the lid on the tube, and slid it into the pocket nearest my heart.

Stripping, I packed my clothes into my bag, alongside the Salmon, my travel toothbrush, my little knife.

I rubbed my naked flesh with the subcutaneous fat of the guillemots.

"Will you not come with me?" I said. "You could return to Ireland by Ryanair. You could rebuild your house, your hall. Or start again…"

"No. I cannot return to the land that betrayed me, to that diminishment. Here, at least, I am lord of my shrinking island." He shrugged. "With its vanishing, I vanish. So be it. I have lived."

I left him then. As I swam the cold water to the shore of England, or perhaps Wales, my bag balanced on my head, I turned once, and looked back: and Charles Haughey waved farewell to his last subject.

Lowering the white thighbone of Dan Bunne, he turned and walked back into the icy cave of his exile: and vanished.

I turned, and swam on.

END OF LEVEL I

The following is a short extract from *Jude: Level 2*, which will be published in hard cover along with Levels 1 and 3 in 2008. In *Level 2*, Jude pursues his True Love through the streets, clubs and brothels of London, and witnesses – among other things – a suicidal (yet highly poetic) parachute jump by the Poet Laureate Andrew Motion, and some rather unorthodox goings on at the Groucho Club. *Level 3* is set in America, where our hero finally uncovers the bizarre truth of his parentage in an extraordinary and apocalyptic finale.

For those who can't wait, *Levels 2* and *3* will be made available online in free instalments from July onwards.

Visit **www.oldstreetpublishing.co.uk** and follow the links to collect your free literary masterpiece.

Jude:

Level 2

ENGLAND

Varnishing Day

"The first quality in a picture is to be a
delight for the eyes.

This does not mean there need be no
sense in it; it is like poetry which, if
it offends the ear, all the sense in the
world will not save from being bad."

-from the final entry in the journal of
Eugène Delacroix, French painter,
1798-1863

THE SNOWY WALK

68.

I came ashore, scraped off the fat, and dressed. I walked up the pebbled beach, and over rocks, and headed inland across rocky fields.

At length I came to a tremendous road, running south-east: to London. I clambered down the embankment, and began to walk toward London along the rough stony path at the road's edge.

As I walked, it began to snow. The flakes falling through the crisp, cold air were firm, and settled on my shoulders and hair without melting. The slush thrown up by the passing trucks, however, threatened to soak and chill me. I stopped, and harvested some of the many plastic bags that gaily adorned the bushes of the embankment. From these fine, waterproof bags I fashioned a crude suit. To allow me to perspire, I incorporated flap-covered slits at the vital points, made with my little knife. Flat against my heart, I made a special pocket, for Angela's lipstick.

An eternal river flowed forward forever at my right hand as

I walked on: vehicles of all sizes, all colours; some tiny, low, and fast, some huge, swaying, sloshing; some with lights flashing; and occasionally my favourites, immense vehicles carrying many other smaller vehicles on their backs.

At the far side of that river was a thin, never-ending island of grass and bushes.

Beyond that island flowed forever toward me a second mighty river, in necessary balance.

That first day's walking, the vein and the artery of the nation's body pulsed in a long, slow rhythm beside me, the great pulse into the city after dawn, the great pulse out of the city as night fell. And at night, the red river of light flowing into the city, the white forever leaving.

Above it all, the high orange lights illuminating the vast road, the vehicles, the swirling orange snow.

In the full of the night, the snow grew heavier and began to drift deeply at the foot of the high embankment to my left, pushing me out into the slowest lane of traffic.

I was encouraged to continue for another hour by the friendly horns of the truck drivers, willing me on with long blasts, but at length I grew too tired to continue.

I harvested another crop of plastic bags from the embankment bushes, and added more layers to my costume until I was as snug and warm as any man in England. Wading uphill, through the deep snow of a deeply drifted drainage gully cut into the embankment, I found the deepest spot and dug a simple snow-hole.

The dense snow above and around me muffled the roar of the river of cars and trucks and vehicles of exotic function. I looked up, along the snow tunnel, at a little patch of sky. I settled my plastic-clad hip into a dip in my snow-bed. Wisps of steam drifted through the slits and from under the flaps of my suit as my perspiration escaped me, into the cold air.

At the tunnel mouth, as the orange clouds cleared, a single star appeared. The star stood steady in the sky as the last snowflakes danced about it and died away. At last it stood, alone.

Imperceptibly, as the world turned, the small star, too, drifted away from me.

Love... love is a puzzler.

The soft, distant swoosh of trucks through slush lulled me at last to sleep.

69.

The next day, I was awoken by the low morning sun shining on my shelter. A light drift of fresh snow had closed the entrance to my snow-hole with a thin crust, so that I opened my eyes in a space as weightless, translucent and featureless as the centre of a pearl.

I stretched and yawned. Perspiration had saturated my clothing in the night but, trapped against me by the plastic, it had warmed agreeably. Comfortable and snug in my layers, I stank pleasantly of myself.

I stood, and broke out through the powdery crust. The sunlight, bouncing off the surrounding snow, dazzled me. Squinting, I walked hip-deep along the gully, down the embankment, toward the deep, roaring rivers of cars, with a great crackling of plastic and crunching of fresh snow. I melted handfuls of the fresh powder in my mouth and drank the clear, pure water. Then I searched through the debris under the snow at the mouth of the gully until I found a large cider bottle, in the traditional amber plastic.

I cut a broad strip from around the bottle with my small knife, then made a notch in the middle for my nose. Notches, then, at either end of the strip for my ears. After a couple of fine adjustments, and the trimming of excess plastic, I had serviceable protection from the glare of the snow, and the risk of snow blindness. The curved plastic clung snugly to the sides of my head.

Little weight rested on my ears, or nose. This was good, for my nose had shrunk in the cold until it was so snub it would have had difficulty supporting my eye-protector unaided. After urinating through a flap in my plastic suit, I rubbed my nose vigorously to make it bigger, and continued my journey.

70.

It was long, hard walking of a kind I hadn't had to do since my Tipperary days. It brought back pleasant memories of rounding up sheep for farmers, on the low hills around the Orphanage, and of herding the sheep along the road into Town, to the Market, or Abattoir. Indeed, my happy memories extended back to a time when the grandparents of those sheep were lambs and I was but a boy.

When I was a young Orphan of nine or ten summers, nothing pleased me and the other young orphans more than to chase and tackle lambs, rolling them over in the long wet grass as they kicked and bucked and bleated, before letting them go, so as to chase them again, till all were exhausted and the Orphans lay down with the Lambs. Then we would usually bite off the testicles of the males, for which we were paid five pence per gonad by the farmer, and an icecream from Father Madrigal for the lad with the greatest haul of Balls at the end of the day. Later, we would play hurling with them until it grew dark and we had lost the last testicle in the long grass. Oh, there is no childhood as happy as the Tipperary childhood!

Although those particular lambs, of course, would not have been the grandparents of the sheep we herded later.

These and other memories filled my heart, and I sang as I walked.

Occasionally, colossal signs warned of tributary streams of

vehicles about to join the great river, within half an hour's walk. Quite why the signs were there I don't know, for I could see and hear the sidestreams joining the mainstream from a good mile away. The great size of the signs indicated they may have been for sight-impaired walkers.

Such tributaries, however, were often the very devil to cross, and I decided at length to walk the more pleasant, landscaped, woodland path that ran between the twin rivers of cars. Unable to find a zebra crossing due to the slush and snow, I decided to trust in the courtesy of the drivers. I began walking across the five rows of traffic that made up the river.

In Tipperary, when walking the little roads, all who knew you would beep their horn and wave as they passed you. I was delighted to discover that, in England, total strangers did the same, one after the other, hundreds of them. The friendliness of the drivers was almost embarrassing, and I tried to wave back individually at everyone who waved at me, which slowed my progress considerably.

Several vehicles were so distracted, waving at me with one hand and beating out a merry tune on their horn with the other, that they mounted the grassy central path, jumped the low strip of metal that ran like a spine along the middle of it, and passed through the bushes into the oncoming river of traffic. These cars were then borne away, backwards, so quickly, whence they had come, that I had no time to return their waves.

Despite these distractions, I finally made the central path. The snow-carpeted grass was pleasant beneath my feet, and I made good time toward London. The occasional tarmacèd breaks in the grassy track were easily crossed, for they seemed rarely used. Trickier were the huge circular islands, many with trees on them, which marked the meeting of rivers, and around which cars swirled clockwise. Fording the broad river to these islands was peculiarly difficult. The planners of the Approach to London, though they had done a lovely job with the landscaped path, seemed not yet

5

to have properly signposted all the necessary Pedestrian Crossings. Without adequate signposting, some of the drivers seemed, quite understandably, under-prepared for the sight of a pedestrian walking out in front of them. But a couple of friendly waves were all it took to sort out these little misunderstandings.

71.

Towards dusk, I started to pick up some of the freshly-slaughtered rabbits which lay along the edge of the river of cars, among the corpses of crows, rats, foxes, hedgehogs, badgers and cats. Most of the freshly killed rabbits had been immediately crushed, recrushed and flattened by subsequent vehicles. However, some had been thrown clear onto the grass by glancing impacts. The best, with their guts unburst and their flesh unbruised, were those rabbits who had merely broken their rear legs, and dragged themselves off the road into the grass to die.

I had so forgotten the lessons of my youth, while living the sophisticated life of Galway City, that I lifted my first rabbit by the ears, to carry it. How the other Orphans would have laughed, could they have seen me! Gravity, of course, caused it to copiously piss down my leg from its death-loosened sphincter. Thankful for my plastic suit, I quickly reversed the rabbit. Sighing, I bent a rear leg back at the joint, to raise the tendon out from the bone, and made a slit behind the raised tendon with my little knife. Tucking the paw of the other leg in behind the tendon, to make a loop of the legs, I carried the rabbit easily on my bent little finger, in the usual manner. I did not wish to carry rabbits in my black bag, due to the fleas, and blood, and excrement. Besides, the narrow strap of my bag, even with the little I was carrying, tended to cut a groove in my shoulder and numb the arms after a while.

Soon I had three good-sized rabbits dangling from my gloved

fingers. I stopped at the next big island, and set up camp. In the heart of the small grove at the centre of the island, I found dry sticks and several types of edible fungus. I gutted and skinned the rabbits, started a fire with flints and dry moss and the steel of my knife, and left rabbits and mushrooms to cook while I built a shelter of branches.

As night fell and the temperature fell with it, great open lorries circled the island, mechanically scattering rock salt into the river of slush, to stop it freezing in the long night. I watched from the central grove, as I slowly ate my baked rabbits, each stuffed with a different variety of wild mushroom.

After sucking the baked marrow from the last of the rabbit bones, I made my way to the edge of the island and searched the shore for the little heaps of rock salt. The drowsy waves of late night traffic swept past me, around the curve of the island and away to London down the great river. Carefully, I collected my salt, and filled my pockets with the discarded plastic cutlery which was abundant on the island's foreshore.

I returned to my little spark of heat, clutching a double handful of whiteness; the hard white cubic crystals of the rocksalt mingled with feathery, brittle crystals of snow. I poured the soft fistfuls onto warm, flat stones at the fire's edge. Soon the heaps slumped, settled for a second, and slumped again. They swiftly halved in size, as the snowflakes collapsed and melted away into a dark puddle on the flat rock. The puddle shrank and drifted off as steam, leaving the small piles of moist salt to dry.

I scraped the skins of the rabbits clean of the last fat with the plastic cutlery. My own little knife was too sharp for this scraping, for I did not wish to nick the skins. The discarded fat and plastic blazed and spat in the fire, giving good light. I carefully and thoroughly massaged the dry salt into the skins, to dry and tan them. As the fire died, I wove a frame from hazel wands, and pegged out the skins to stretch and cure.

Before I slept, I took the lipstick from the pocket by my heart and removed the top. I took out the brittle yellow triangle of paper. I read it again by the glow of the dying fire in the heart of the glade – the mysterious clue to my origins: Gents… Anal… Cruise…

As I read, I wafted the open lipstick beneath my nose, its feminine perfume dizzying me so that the letters blurred before my eyes. How strange, that mere chemistry could have gender. Inhaling these volatile oils, a female figure shimmered at the edge of vision, at the far side of the fire. Beyond the warm, trembling air, the dark became a woman.

Carefully, I put it all away.

At length I fell asleep, the lipstick moving with my heart.

In the morning, the skins and frame were easily carried on my back. As I walked, the skins cured slowly in the sun and wind. Once they were cured, dry and supple, I could take them from the frame. A few more days. I would sew them then, with bone needles, and with sinew and tendon as my strong thread.

72.

In a few days, I had a jacket of rabbit fur, lined with rabbit fur.

By the end of a week, I had a suit. For variety, I added hardwearing badger trim at hem and cuff. My amber goggles I lined at the nose-notch and ear-notches with white rabbit fur, from the soft belly of a young rabbit, sewn neatly to the plastic. First, using a wire heated orange in the fire, I melted sewing holes in the plastic. The wire slid through with a hiss, leaving a raised rim of molten plastic around each hole to cool & set into a reinforcing eyelet. Then I sewed on the shaped strips of skin using the bone needle & the delicate but strong front leg tendons. The warmth of the soft fur, and its gentle caress, caused my nose to maintain a decent size on even the coldest morning. The goggles sat better, and I was pleased.

Occasionally I was reminded by a warmth in my belly of the hidden presence of the Ring Babette had given me. Deep in my navel, at my precise centre of gravity, it seemed to gain energy from my walk.

Once, I woke in the night and saw a white light shining from within my navel, illuminating the branches above me, bright leaves and hard shadows. As I woke, and tried to focus, the light faded to a dim pale green and dimmed again to a deep blue, and went out.

Steadily, I progressed towards London.